ELLORA'S CAVEMEN

DREAMS OF THE OASIS

ELLORA'S CAVE
ROMANTICA PUBLISHING

An Ellora's Cave Romantica Publication

www.ellorascave.com

Ellora's Cavemen: Dreams of the Oasis III

ISBN # 1419954539
ALL RIGHTS RESERVED.
Pleasuremaid Copyright © 2006 Cricket Starr
Tempt Me Twice Copyright © 2006 Renee Luke
Werewolf in L.A. Copyright © 2006 Marianne LaCroix
Priestess of Desire Copyright © 2006 Mary Winter
Summer Lovin' Copyright © 2006 Shelley Munro
Interplanetary Survival Episode #495 Copyright © 2006 Tielle St.
Clare

Edited by Raelene Gorlinsky.
Cover design by Darrell King. Photography by Dennis Roliff.

Electronic book Publication September 2006
Trade Paperback Publication September 2006

Warning:

The following material contains graphic sexual content meant for mature readers. This story has been rated E–rotic by a minimum of three independent reviewers.

Ellora's Cave Publishing offers three levels of Romantica™ reading entertainment: S (S-ensuous), E (E-rotic), and X (X-treme).

S-*ensuous* love scenes are explicit and leave nothing to the imagination.

E-*rotic* love scenes are explicit, leave nothing to the imagination, and are high in volume per the overall word count. In addition, some E-rated titles might contain fantasy material that some readers find objectionable, such as bondage, submission, same sex encounters, forced seductions, and so forth. E-rated titles are the most graphic titles we carry; it is common, for instance, for an author to use words such as "fucking", "cock", "pussy", and such within their work of literature.

X-*treme* titles differ from E-rated titles only in plot premise and storyline execution. Unlike E-rated titles, stories designated with the letter X tend to contain controversial subject matter not for the faint of heart.

Ellora's Cavemen:
Dreams of the Oasis III

PLEASUREMAID

Cricket Starr

Chapter One

ဆ

She was cold. So very, very cold. Shivering, the woman pulled herself to a sitting position and raised her head. Something liquid fell into her face and slid down the back of her neck.

She identified it. *Water. Rain.* Cold and wet, and she was outside, sitting on the ground. Her fingers on one hand stung and when she looked at them, there were pale red marks on the tips. Even as she watched the marks faded to thin lines, although the sting from them remained.

Rain dripped from her hair into her face.

She brushed the hair aside and a light caught her attention, just past the neatly trimmed bushes that surrounded her. She struggled to her feet and headed toward it.

Light meant warmth and shelter from the rain, and she needed both. She clutched her arms around herself trying to preserve what body heat she had.

It seemed to take forever, moving slowly across the thick plush of the ground cover—some sort of short grass, well tended and soft beneath her bare feet.

Why aren't I wearing shoes? Why was her only garment a simple shift—thin, sleeveless and barely reaching her knees, of no use in weather like this?

So many questions and no answers—she needed answers. The light she'd noticed was over a door set in a wall with a roof overhang. The wall of a building, large and imposing. She reached the door and for a brief moment gloried in the overhang that kept the rain off her. She found and held down the buzzer.

After a long time the door opened, revealing someone. She registered a man, tall, broad-shouldered, and dressed in a sleeping robe. His eyes...there was something about his eyes...she knew him.

He looked at her quizzically. "Who are you?"

She opened her mouth...and realized she had no answer for him. She knew him but not herself. She had no idea who she was.

It was one question too many — the world spun and she collapsed.

* * * * *

Gall stared down at the damp bundle of woman on the floor and wondered at what was going on in his life. During the past two years he'd had a total of barely a dozen visitors and certainly none like the unconscious woman at his feet.

Of everyone, he preferred the woman. Even soaking wet and with her silvery hair plastered to her scalp, she was still nicer to look at than the old men who made up his father's council.

But nice as she was to look at she couldn't stay where she was. Her body blocked the doorway and the rain was blowing in. Gall lifted her so he could shut the door.

She settled into his arms with a sweet sigh, as nice to hold as she was to look at. A bit small, but curvy. Very wet, though, particularly her hair and dress, which clung to both of them, and her skin felt like ice. A deep shiver ran through her and he clutched her closer.

Whoever she was she'd get sick if she stayed like this. He needed to get her warmed up and the heated bathing pool in his quarters would be the best cure for that. Gall hoisted her higher and headed that way.

She was still unconscious when he got her to the tub and that gave him pause. He couldn't just put her in this way. He'd need to hold her head above water and it would be best to get in with her. Of course he couldn't keep on his robe...

Get in the tub naked with a beautiful woman? *What a darn shame that was!*

A grin on his face, he slipped off his sandals and robe and stepped into the heated water, still holding his insensible bundle. Her gown was already soaked and would take no further harm.

He settled onto the tub's seat and let her head rest against his shoulder. Her shivering gradually quieted, and after a moment her eyes opened. Gall startled at the look of them…like golden pools with a black iris in the middle, surrounded by lashes the same pale silver as her hair. Her lips parted, and she breathed in, a startled reaction to being in his arms.

Then she breathed out, and Gall caught the sweetness of her breath. It was like a drug, heavy and enticing. He took it deep into his lungs and his cock, already interested at having a woman so close, now hardened and throbbed.

He clutched her closer, pulling so her bottom rested against his lap. The feel of her buttocks against his cock was a sweet torture though the thin fabric of her gown.

She floated next to him, and her arms went around his neck. Her lips were just within reach. Gall closed his mouth over them.

A kiss. Just a kiss but when was the last time he'd tasted anything as sweet as this? If he'd thought her breath was intoxicating, her lips made him drunk. She opened her mouth to his probing tongue and he couldn't think.

He could barely keep himself from tearing her clothes from her and throwing her onto the marble floor of his bath, thrusting himself deep within her. It had been a long time since he'd had a woman so enticing beside him.

But he did no such thing. He forced his hands to be gentle, to strip away the thin gown with care. She seemed almost childlike—her eyes stared at him with no guile within them. He would not be forceful with her.

Her gaze might have been innocent, but there was nothing but woman in the heavy breasts he found under her garment, the nipples the most tempting pink he'd ever seen. Gall captured one of them with his mouth, and she arched against him. He suckled her and she cried out, her hand holding his head to her.

Hesitation disappeared at her welcoming response. She no longer shivered against him and the skin that had been like ice now seemed to burn. Gall slid her across his lap so his cock was poised just outside her opening. He thrust up through the water and speared her. She made a small sound of surprise and appreciation and her golden eyes were the size of saucers when he looked at her.

Her pussy was tight, hot and welcoming. He lifted his hips and drove deeper within her, then pulled back. Her arms tightened around his neck and she moaned, a long heartfelt sigh of appreciation.

He picked a rhythm that seemed to suit them both, the water undulating around them. Not too fast. The feel of her around his cock was that of a well-fitting glove and he wanted to enjoy that for as long as he could. It would be over too soon, he knew.

The pace he picked was perfect. She lifted her head and stared at him with those golden eyes of hers and he could see her approaching climax. Gall couldn't help his smile. He wanted to see her come, feel her climax while he was still in her. He sped up and she clutched at him, now driving herself onto his hard cock.

She was perfect in his arms and all he wanted was to keep doing this forever. Not likely—if only he could make her come before he did. He wanted to delay the inevitable.

But as her first wave of climax started, her pussy pulled at him and that was his undoing. He held off as long as he could, but even though she wasn't quite at her peak the urge to pull out of her became impossible to ignore.

She was still riding his cock when he grabbed her hips and with force pulled her off him. Gall lifted her onto the marble edging as, with a curse, he gave in to the orgasm he'd resisted.

Free of her, his cock discharged its load into the water.

Shock showed in her face. Shock and confusion. Gall steeled himself for the anger he knew would follow. Even the carefully trained courtesans charged with servicing him during the past two years had been unable to hide their displeasure when he'd pulled out of them like that. Finally he'd told his keepers to send no more of them. Better he service himself.

But this woman said nothing and as he watched concern filled her eyes. Her hand caressed his face.

"Why did you do that?"

Her soft question was almost harder to take than her anger would have been. He found himself telling her the truth.

"I...I was given a compulsion. I can't climax inside a woman...it's—it's to keep me from fathering any children."

"Oh."

He'd waited for her to ask why, but at her simple acceptance of his condition, something inside Gall released. Whoever this woman was, he liked that more than anything. "My name is Gall." He wouldn't burden her with the rest of his names for now.

For an instant she tensed and something like panic was in her eyes, but then her expression changed to one of relief and her lips curved into a smile. "I am Dina."

* * * * *

Dina's pleasure at getting at least one memory back nearly overwhelmed her. At least now she knew her name and that meant that whatever had happened to her, the damage probably wasn't permanent.

So—she had a name but still couldn't remember her purpose...but she knew it had something to do with Gall. Once she'd smelled the man and tasted his lips, she'd known he was connected to why she was there.

Wrapped in a towel Dina watched as Gall sorted through his clothes, finding a long sleeveless tunic for her to wear. She couldn't keep her eyes off him. Tall and broad-shouldered, his body was all molded muscle. His face was that of a young god, dark-haired, with eyes so black they seemed made of stone.

But they weren't hard like stone. They danced with humor when he saw how big his garment was on her.

"You look like a child dressed in your big brother's clothes."

"I'm not a child," she told him saucily.

"No, you aren't." His lips curled up with sensual male interest and her core heated as his gaze raked over her body. "You are most definitely a woman. And I bet you are hungry."

She wasn't but she said nothing as he went off in search of food for them. At least she wasn't hungry for food. Her purpose here definitely had something to do with Gall.

She was here...to take care of him? No, that didn't seem quite right. To have sex with him, certainly. Once she'd woken up with his hands on her that had been all she could think about.

And it had been great up until he'd ended it so abruptly. He'd said he couldn't climax inside a woman...a compulsion. Perhaps she was here to help him with that?

Dina nibbled one of her fingernails, pulling it away when she realized how much shorter it was than the others. Chewing her nails must be a nervous habit of hers.

Great. All she wanted was to know who she was and her purpose. She knew her name was Dina, that she wanted sex with Gall, and that she bit her nails. It wasn't much but at least now she was warm and dry and that was a lot better than being in a cold wet garden after falling off a wall...

Wall? Dina startled. Was that how she got into Gall's garden, by climbing over the wall surrounding it? Was the fall the reason for her memories being scrambled?

But why would she be sneaking in?

Gall's return ended her introspection. He held a platter of something that smelled wonderful and her stomach lurched in anticipation.

Dina smiled at him. "I guess I am hungry."

Chapter Two

৪০

She had a good appetite, Gall noticed. He also enjoyed watching her eat. Every mouthful seemed to be an experiment, every taste a sensual delight for her. Only a few items didn't seem to meet her expectations and she only tried them once.

Dina tried the wine he brought but apparently that also wasn't to her taste. She preferred the fruit juice instead.

Gall watched her eat and wondered. Who was she and why was she here? Even more, what should he do about it? In truth he should have called his guards as soon as she'd arrived. It was against the rules for her to be here.

Perhaps that's why he didn't want to notify them. After all this time he didn't want to follow their rules any longer. He wanted this woman and he knew they'd take her from him, saying it was for his protection.

Ha! If anything she needed protection from him. Even after their earlier session in the tub he was interested in making love again. At least as much lovemaking as he was permitted to do.

Not for the first time, Gall bridled at the restrictions that had been put on his life. He'd been falsely accused. For them to lock him up, and, even worse, saddle him with that wretched compulsion…the first thing he'd do if he ever got out of here would be to see if there weren't some way to have that removed.

He really wanted to make proper love to a woman…starting with Dina.

She looked up and smiled at him. "I bet you're thinking about sex again."

"Would it surprise you if I said yes?"

"Not really. It would just mean that we are thinking very similar thoughts." She slid her hand up under his robe and found his cock, hard and ready again. "See, I told you sex was on your mind."

With a beautiful woman like Dina around, why wouldn't it be? He couldn't get over how wonderful she smelled. All he wanted to do was draw her close and make love all night long. Trouble was that he'd never be able to finish what he started.

Better he not start at all. He drew away from her. "Perhaps this isn't such a great idea."

"Are you worried about what happened before?" she asked softly.

He let his silence answer. Dina tilted her head as if in thought. "You say you can't come inside a woman...but what about inside her mouth? You couldn't make her pregnant that way."

In her mouth? Gall shook his head. "I haven't tried that."

Intrigued Gall watched her open his robe and free his cock, already weeping its interest. She smiled and gave it several long strokes. He lay back and signaled her permission to continue.

Dina poised over his cock, the too-large neckline of her tunic dipping low enough for him to see her breasts. He licked his lips only to see her mimic the gesture, just before she gave a tentative lick to the broad head of his penis.

It felt so good, he couldn't help his moan. Encouraged she took the tip into her mouth and this time he didn't even fight a groan. So hot and inviting was her mouth. He felt like he could stay in there all day. Her teeth rasped softly against the ridge under the tip, and she sucked the tip a little.

The top of his head nearly came off. "Please, more," he begged.

She gave him more, and then more again. Gall's stomach tightened with each draw of her mouth on him, each little suck, each sweet bite. She did it over and over, and Gall's hands clutched the sheets of the bed. Her mouth was so good...perfect.

His stomach clenched, his balls growing heavier. He was coming...he should pull out...he should...

But she didn't let him and she sucked him deeper into her mouth, and...

And then he was coming, hard, into the back of her throat. Her name was a soft prayer on his lips followed by his cry of ecstasy.

Dina made a quiet noise as if she were choking and then he felt her swallow, taking his cum into her.

She sat up, licking her lips like a cat with cream, her face showing the same satisfaction. Gall gathered her into his arms and then they were both on the bed, Dina held next to him. For the first time in years he felt the satisfied weariness of sexual completion.

"I didn't do anything for you," he whispered in her ear.

Dina raised her head to kiss him, her mouth sweet against his. "I'm fine for now. You are tired—let's sleep."

Sleep sounded so good. He pulled her close and let the world drift away.

* * * * *

Dina listened to Gall's breathing even out and knew he slept. She still held his taste in her mouth, tart and familiar. Warmth filled her...satisfaction at having given him pleasure.

That's what she was here for. That's why they'd sent her...

They'd sent her? Uneasiness rose in Dina as another memory fell into place. She'd been sent here, by someone, but who and for what purpose? Sent to climb over a tall stone wall, to get inside his room. Sent with Gall's face in her mind and his taste and smell in her memory.

Sent to satisfy his needs—or perhaps to cure him of his compulsion? Maybe...but as Dina nestled deeper into his arms, she wished she was sure. Somehow she wondered if a darker purpose hadn't been intended. Why else would she have had to sneak in?

But it was a secret Gall wanted to keep as well. The next morning he had her hide in a closet while a maidservant cleaned the room and bath. Later he told her that he needed to keep her presence a secret. There were those who would make her leave if they found her.

Dina didn't want to leave and so sat in the dark stuffy closet as quietly as possible while Gall joked with the maid and someone else, a man with the gruff manner of a soldier.

A soldier guarding whom, she wondered—Gall, or the maidservant? The woman commented on Gall's good humor, and commented aloud on what he was so happy about.

Dina wondered if it might be due to her presence. Gall needed a regular lover and in the absence of other instructions that was the purpose she'd given herself. Something inside her craved a purpose.

She wanted to please him. This morning they'd tried to make love again, but he'd interrupted it as suddenly as he had in the tub. It had bothered her only a little, but she read Gall's frustration when he'd had to stop before climaxing inside her.

Finally she'd taken him into her mouth again, and this time he'd finished, even easier than before without trying to pull out. So his mind had accepted oral sex as acceptable. It was probably because the compulsion that gripped him had been linked to sex that could produce children.

That gave her another idea to explore later. She hoped to desensitize him to making love, decoupling it from procreation in his mind...then perhaps the compulsion could be banished completely.

Once his rooms had been cleaned, Gall let her out of the closet. He pulled a games board off a shelf, along with a box of carved pieces.

"I don't suppose you know how to play Castles."

She had to shake her head, but that didn't faze him. Instead he set out the board on the low table.

"It isn't like there is that much else for us to do," he said then, at her smile, gave a little laugh. "Well, other than *that*. But we can't stay in bed all day. I'll teach you."

Chapter Three

❧

The lesson went into the early evening. As it turned out, Gall was a fanatical player who loved the game and knew all its nuances. Thankfully he was also an excellent teacher. Faced with something new to study, Dina cheerfully threw herself into learning everything about the game that he could teach her.

They played all afternoon broken only by her returning to her closet hiding place whenever a guard made a sweep of the rooms. She realized that Gall wasn't afraid of the gruff-sounding men. He seemed more annoyed by them than anything else.

Later in the day a servant came with Gall's dinner, which he told the man to stow in the kitchen rather than serve it right away.

The food was fortunately quite plentiful as he shared it later with her. It was also delicious, the best she'd ever eaten…at least as far as she could remember. Dina still couldn't remember much from before waking on the grass outside Gall's home.

Bits and pieces came to her. A remembered taste, a smell that triggered a memory. But too much still remained hidden. She'd told Gall the truth, that she'd fallen off the wall and couldn't remember who or what she was, and he'd accepted it.

She hadn't. How was it that she'd come to this place? Sure, she'd climbed over the wall that she could now see through the vegetation lining the edges of the yard. Way at the top she saw a wire and a memory came of sudden intense pain.

But why had she climbed the wall? What had been her reason?

Plus the wall seemed forbiddingly high. Was she truly so gifted a climber to have taken it on or had someone helped her up on the other side? If so…who would have done such a thing?

21

Again too many questions. Whenever they became too much, Dina would look at Gall, breathe deeply of his wonderful sensual scent and let desire overwhelm the questions in her mind.

It was enough that she was here, with him. It was enough that he was hers to smile with, eat with, and challenge him at his favorite game. The answers to why she was here could wait.

It was enough that she was.

Every meal, every game, every conversation they had made her happy. From the way his initial reserve gradually gave way to warmth and smiles, her presence made him happy as well. The day passed with their growing closer together, until by nightfall they might have known each other from childhood.

Dina realized uncomfortably that she had no memories of any time spent as a child. It was as if she'd arrived at Gall's door fully grown into the world. Dina shuddered when that thought occurred to her and she wondered why.

Fortunately it didn't seem to occur to Gall. After a while Dina realized that he asked no uncomfortable questions of her, of whether she remembered anything of who she was or how she'd gotten here. He seemed to accept that she didn't know the answers.

He didn't seem to care, either. It appeared to be enough for him that she'd found her way here. What mattered to him was that she laughed when he made a joke, and teased him into good humor when he was glum, and loved having sex with him, even though he couldn't complete the act.

And that she played Castles. Gall loved playing Castles almost as much as he did making love.

He had one game strategy he was very fond of and used frequently in their practice games. Late that evening they were playing and she waited until she saw him set up for it. With a smile Dina moved her cavalry piece to thwart him, laughing at the surprise in his face.

Gall stared at her for a moment then joined her laughter.

"You've learned enough about this game for tonight, little mystery woman. Let's play a different game."

He pulled her into his arms and Dina surrendered to his kiss. Warm, sweet, and demanding. Gall kissed the way he played Castles...intensely and with the ambition to win.

But not just that. He played because he enjoyed the game and wanted to share that. In the game of sex the same ambition was there.

Gall wasn't satisfied to have his own needs met. He needed to satisfy her as well.

It wasn't that hard. All he had to do was touch her and desire swept through her. The touch of his lips burned, the swipe of a fingertip left a frisson of need that always settled in her groin.

He worshiped her breasts, nibbling the tips with gentle teeth and lips, sucking with soft intent. Each of her orbs seemed to swell, the nipples hardening into tender points. Each pull on a nipple spiraled down through her belly to center into her core.

Their clothes came off in quick succession and soon Dina was kneeling on the bed next to him. He entered her from behind, his hands caressing her back and coming to settle on her buttocks, kneading each gently.

Each deep thrust drove her closer to fulfillment, but as the wave built inside her, she sensed his discomfort rise as well. He was going to pull out of her again, before he reached climax himself.

She could feel it...and this time she didn't want it to happen that way.

Before the compulsion seized him, she pulled away from him, releasing his cock to dangle behind her. Gall groaned.

She didn't allow him to wallow in self-pity. Instead she looked over her shoulder at him, lifting her ass higher and wiggling it invitingly.

"There is more than one way to make love, Gall, and some carry no risk of pregnancy."

He stared at her for a long moment before apparently catching her drift. "You wish to do that…with me?"

"I want you to come inside me, my love. However that can be done."

He hesitated a minute more. "I don't want to hurt you."

"It doesn't hurt for me," she lied, not knowing if it was the truth. She couldn't remember having a man's cock in her ass, but who was to say that she hadn't…and that it had not caused her pain?

Gall raised her hips closer and his hand explored again the round mounds of her bottom. He reached forward to cup her sex, using his fingers on her clit to drive her crazy. She leaned into his hand, letting her ass rise higher in the air.

Gall leaned forward and spread the globules with his other hand, the first still pleasuring her. He poked a tentative finger into the tiny puckered opening.

Dina jerked further into his pleasuring hand, the sensation of being entered anally even by a fingertip sending shock waves through her. Some pain…and something that wasn't pain that she really wanted to explore. She knew immediately this was new for her, but it felt right anyway. She knew it was the right approach to take with Gall.

She looked over her shoulder and noted that Gall's face showed an intense fascination. From a drawer he produced a small vial of oil, which he used with a practiced hand on his cock, smoothing it on with long strokes. His eyes closed in pleasure, and Dina smiled. This was how he'd been satisfying his needs all this time.

Then he took the oil and worked a small amount into her tight opening. It made the opening slick and smooth and easier for him to enter. He let his finger mimic the action of his cock, loosening her up until he was able to work a second finger in, then a third. Dina groaned with each additional insertion but assured him he was causing her no harm.

In truth he wasn't. As three fingers now stretched her well-lubed opening, Dina cried out, an orgasm swamping her.

Gall took his cock in hand and fitted it with the now relaxed opening and thrust through it, just the head, letting her body learn to accept him. Now when she glanced back, she saw the sweat beading on his brow, his finely developed chest gleaming with forced patience. He grabbed her hips and pulled her toward him, slowly letting more of his cock fill her.

Dina's moan was heartfelt and it was all she could do not to simply impale herself further onto him. The oil had made the head of his cock slick and easy to accept. Now he reached to her channel to gather her liquid arousal and slide that along his shaft, working some of it into her opening, using her natural lubrication in addition to the oil. He thrust and he was embedded deep within her, panting with the exertion of taking so slow an entry.

Such control Gall had. Dina wondered at it. She could see that it took all his strength to hold still and let her finish acclimating herself to his presence.

Then his control snapped and Gall pushed her forward to rest on her elbows, then back again, his hips pistoning in time. Now they were truly joined.

"So tight, so hot, and good," Gall said, his voice broken and harsh with passion and need. Each thrust put him closer to completion, and this time when she felt him tense, she did not get the feeling he would pull out.

This time he'd be able to stay within her to climax.

And he did. Just as she thought that, he froze in place, his breath a hot breeze against her back.

"I'm coming in you, Dina. Coming…coming!" The last was a long scream and then she felt him push hard inside her and his cock jerked, throbbed, and heat from his cum shot deep into her backside channel.

Dina climaxed as well, between the heat in her ass and his fingers still massaging her clit. She bucked and her ass milked him and it seemed like he came again, still inside her.

Gall threw his arms around her waist, burying his face in her back, nuzzling her hair.

"That was amazing," he whispered.

It had been, and it had been successful. Dina smiled at him.

"I can't wait to try your pussy again. This time, I think I can stay inside." He hesitated. "Dina...I am so glad you are here...I want to keep you beside me forever. If that could be arranged, would you agree?"

Sudden joy made it hard to speak. She felt the same for him and wanted to tell him so. Only something made her stop and wait.

This had happened so fast...she still didn't understand just who she was and why she was here. Worse, she didn't know what was going to become of them. She couldn't stay hidden in his closet forever and soon someone would figure out she was here. When that happened they'd be separated and somehow she knew that if they committed to loving each other it would only make things worse when that happened.

She did love him but there was still so much wrong with their situation.

He seemed to read her thoughts and something in him stilled. "I know there are a hundred reasons you should say no, Dina. We haven't known each other very long. You can't remember why you are here. I haven't told you why I'm locked up. Not that I want to tell you, but I can say that I'm innocent of what they accused me of."

Finally she found something to say. "You are a prisoner, then."

"Yes." He ran a finger down her face. "I don't want to lose you, Dina. For the first time in two years...actually longer than that, I don't feel alone. I want to keep you with me."

He lay back on the bed, rubbing his jaw, his face showing his frustration. "There must be something we can do to keep you here. Maybe I could ask my father...or my brother." Gall's laugh was bitter. "On second thought that's probably not such a good idea. It was his idea to saddle me with that compulsion. The last thing he'd want is to see me able to perform with a woman now."

Dina wanted to ask why his brother would have done so treacherous a thing, but she didn't. Instead she took Gall's hand and kissed it. "If you could keep me, I would live with you."

Gall's face lit up. "I think I could very well fall in love with you."

She couldn't help but smile. "I know I love you...that's why I want to stay."

He leaned in to seal the bargain with a kiss until a rap on the door, caught their attention.

"Who could be here this late?" Gall muttered. He grabbed his clothes off the floor and dressed. "Stay in the bed, Dina. I'll be back."

She couldn't help her fear, though and rose to stand behind the door, listening as Gall exclaimed a greeting to their midnight visitor.

"Himla? What makes you sneak in here at this time of night?"

A sense of danger came to her, which was reinforced by the stranger's first words.

"I came because I've heard there is a threat to your safety."

Chapter Four

∞

A threat to Gall? Acting with an instinct she didn't think about, Dina pulled on her thigh, uncovering a seam built into the skin. She tugged and it separated, revealing a narrow slit in her flesh—and a super-thin twelve-centimeter crystal blade hidden inside the muscle of her leg.

The presence of the weapon troubled her. Why did she have a hidden knife and how had she known it was there? Even so, she wanted it, to protect Gall if necessary. Dina shoved the question aside and pulled the knife, noting how familiar it felt in her hand.

Hefting it, Dina peeked through the crack in the door at the newcomer. A friend of Gall's, she could sense that, even though there seemed to be a lot of tension between the two men. An old friend, but not one who'd been to visit during Gall's imprisonment, she guessed. She used the rest of her senses to tell her about him.

His face showed guilt, shame, and anger, but the latter wasn't directed at Gall...he wasn't the threat she sensed. She eased the slender crystal blade back into its hiding place and resealed the skin over it.

"A threat to me here?" Gall scoffed. "I couldn't get hurt even if I tried."

"There have been rumors about an attempted assassination of you...and other things as well."

Gall's laugh was bitter. "Why kill me when I'm in here? I might as well be dead already."

"You know the evidence you were convicted on seemed overwhelmingly against you, but now there are doubts. Nothing substantial...nothing we can use as proof you were framed."

The newcomer's frustration was genuine. "What I'm hearing now is if it can be proved you aren't guilty, then you'll be freed and that seems to be a threat to someone. It could even be that your brother is involved…that the attempt to kill him was just a plot to discredit you…"

"Gratus faked an assassination just to get rid of me?" Gall was outraged, but almost as quickly he calmed and Dina could see that the idea meant something to him. He rubbed his jaw and looked troubled. "That would explain a lot."

"I came because I needed to apologize. I should have known better. If I can help in any way…"

"There is no need. You were the last to abandon me and the first to seek me out now." As he did when he played Castles, Gall continued to rub his chin, obviously strategizing.

"Here is what we'll do. Get the evidence we need to clear me and get me out of here, Himla. That's what you can do."

"I'll do my best." His friend paused a moment. "You are my prince, Galleanus Ell Vanant and I pledge loyalty. I'll be in the guest quarters." He left, Gall staring after him, a look of hope in his expression.

Dina sank to the floor. Like a flood, memories came back to her. She knew the name, knew who he was. Prince Galleanus of the planet Vanant, a hereditary monarchy on the outskirts of the galaxy. His father was king, his brother the crown prince, and Gall was the second son, disgraced and banished to a hidden prison for attempted murder of king's heir. Convicted but not guilty, she knew.

Not guilty because she knew who was…because she was part of the conspiracy against him!

She reached up to the back of her head and found the small, almost impossible to notice input jacks buried under a skin flap in her scalp. That plus the hidden pocket in her flesh made it clear what she was and all the questions she'd had assembled in her mind lined up like soldiers alongside their matching answers.

Who was she? She was Dina, a synthetic human created and programmed for a specific purpose.

Whose purpose? Not hers...those who had sent her here.

Who were they? A name came to her, as well as a face—Prince Gratus, the brother Gall was supposed to have conspired against.

And why? Because it hadn't been enough to frame Gall and lock him away. She knew now her purpose, and that of the knife.

Dina returned to bed before Gall entered the room, pretending to sleep as he lay down beside her and wrapped his body around hers. Eventually he muttered into her neck and his breathing evened out.

She couldn't tell him what she knew. Not now. It was still too fresh and she needed to think.

No more questions now. Dina had wanted to know who she was and what purpose she had. She now knew both but she didn't like the answers. One thing confused her...why hadn't she already killed him? She'd had ample opportunity. The programming they'd given her should have activated before now, forcing her to embed the knife into his heart.

But she'd hurt her hand on the wire at the top of the fence and lost her memory. She flexed her fingers at the remembered pain. Somehow that had stopped her.

What to do now? His friend Himla said they needed evidence to prove Gall's innocence. She could give it to them...names and faces she remembered, the fact of what she was, her presence here, and the knife in her thigh—proof of the conspiracy.

She couldn't give it to Gall. Inside her heart ached over deceiving him, but she couldn't face telling him the truth.

He'd said he thought he loved her. She was synth...not someone to love.

When she knew Gall slept, Dina slid from his arms and crept from the bed. For a moment she watched him, heart breaking over what she needed to do. Now she knew what the ache she'd felt meant when she looked at him. It meant she loved him.

For a moment she was almost glad she hadn't said the words that would have bound them together. Her hesitation hadn't been in error.

She'd thought her purpose was to love him. But she'd been wrong. It had been to kill him, but she'd fallen in love anyway.

She could keep her silence and stay with him for as long as they could be together. But that would be wrong. Gall deserved better than the half-life he was living.

Dina took a shuddering breath. Her purpose was no longer to kill him or to love him. It was to save him from his enemies and set him free.

Silently she left to find his friend and give him the proof he needed.

* * * * *

Gall gazed through the one-way glass in the observation chamber of the palace interrogation room. Dina sat on the narrow bed in the adjacent room, head bowed, face blank. Now that he knew the truth, he could see the signs of what she was — the inhumanly even tone of her skin and the silky sameness of her hair color.

No blemishes, moles, freckles, or scars marred that perfect skin. There were no tiny lines from laughing or frowning to crease her face. She was perfect because she'd been designed to be that way, grown fully formed within a few weeks and not years, programmed to be a person in only a day. No history marked her as it did normal people.

Dina was synthetic — a manufactured human with memories and thoughts programmed into her.

Too perfect — too inhuman. Gall kept his face composed but inside he was dying. He'd fallen in love with a synth, a woman he couldn't keep.

She spoke, answering the question posed her by the interrogator, her voice an even, emotionless monotone. "I didn't remember at first why I was there. I thought…" Her voice trailed off for a second, and Gall thought he saw her chest heave with suppressed emotion. "I thought I was there to please him."

"Please him?"

"Give him pleasure." She raised her hand and her finger strayed to her mouth. Absently she chewed on the nail, and Gall suddenly remembered her doing that at his home. Nibbling her fingernail.

"You were programmed to kill him."

The accusation came in a flat monotone. She answered in the same way. "Yes."

"Why didn't you?"

"I didn't remember my mission. I…" Her voice broke. "In the climb over the wall I caught my hand on the electrified wire." She held up her hand, showing the thin scars across the fingertips. "I didn't remember anything at first. But his smell, his voice…"

Her questioner came into view, holding a shirt. Gall recognized it as one of his that hadn't returned from the laundry.

"You were given this to learn his smell. Played recordings of his voice and shown his picture. You were imprinted on him to be his slayer."

Dina's face lifted and while her face stayed impassive, her eyes seemed to glint with unshed tears. "Yes."

The other man showed her pictures and she identified them. "I remember this one and this. They were there."

"Your brother's men." Himla's voice came over Gall's shoulder. "We didn't believe it at first, but this is proof. Your brother sent that assassin synth in to kill you."

"But she didn't," he found himself saying.

"No. As she said, she was damaged in entering and her primary function kicked in instead." Himla gave a short bark of a laugh. "Lucky you, she was a pleasuremaid."

His sweet little Dina, a reprogrammed pleasuremaid made into an assassin. Gall shook his head.

The other man gave him a curious look. "I've heard good talk about those things. How was it in bed?"

"She," Gall said firmly. Dina might be a synth, but she was no object, not in his opinion. But then he didn't have the words to describe how it had been to make love with her. Her infinite patience and skill, her sweetness and sexual inventiveness, the latter of which had finally removed the blocks in his mind about lovemaking.

"She was perfect," was all he said finally.

He could feel Himla's gaze boring into him and the speculation in it. "I guess she was. Too bad they're going to have to dismantle her."

Gall spun around. "What do you mean? They can't kill her!"

"She's damaged, your highness. Unreliable. Programmed for one thing, then another…who knows what she's capable of?"

"She could have killed me, but she didn't. I can't let her die in return."

Himla stared at him. "It isn't like it's a real woman, Gall."

He gritted his teeth. The old prejudice against synthetic humans — one he would have agreed with just two days ago, but now… "She's real enough for me."

"Of course she's real!" A small bewhiskered man with white hair and an impatient air bustled over to them. He took a long look at the woman through the glass. "One of my best works, too. I spent a lot of time on her kind."

Gall swung to face him. "You made Dina?" Inside him something cringed. More proof she wasn't the woman he thought she was.

"I'm Dr. Lassa—I designed the line," he said proudly. "A highly limited group, each an individual. No cookie-cutter synths where they all look and sound alike. Like her sisters, she's one of a kind and perfect." He frowned as she raised her hand and nibbled her nail. "Except for that. This one has always had that nervous habit."

"I didn't think synths had habits," Himla said.

The old man shook his head. "Of course they do. They are humans, just like us. Just not born the same way."

"But preprogrammed to be slaves," Himla said. "At the whim of whoever controls them. Like this one was."

The man muttered angrily. "I didn't authorize what happened to her—she was stolen from our laboratory. The programming is only a result of those who don't want to see artificial humans with free will." He spoke to Gall. "Your Dina is different. She broke through her conditioning to warn you of the plot against your life."

Gall considered that. Dina had come forward to warn him, and she had to have known what the result would be. Synths had no rights and could be destroyed.

Himla wasn't convinced. "You can't let her get close to you, Gall. You don't know what she's capable of."

"She was capable of love."

"She's a pleasuremaid—it's programmed into her. As soon as she was given your scent she locked in on it and would do anything to please you. It isn't real, Gall."

Wasn't it real? They'd spent just two days together and yet he'd thought he'd known her better than any other woman. But he hadn't. If he had, she would have told him directly what she was and why she was there. Instead he'd heard it from Himla after waking to find her gone.

Perhaps he did love her but she wasn't what he'd thought her to be and his friend was right. With Gratus discredited, he'd have to take the role of crown prince and he couldn't afford a liaison with a woman he couldn't trust.

Slowly he shook his head. "Get the evidence we need from her, Himla. Make sure we can prove my brother is responsible and clear my name. And then..." His voice trailed off. Dina looked at the glass wall between them, as if she could see through it, as if she knew he was on the other side. She looked sad and lost, but resigned.

That image of her would haunt him forever, he knew. She'd saved him, both from his brother and his imprisonment. Even more, she'd saved him from the despair he'd been mired in, and more—she'd returned his sexuality to him.

He'd fallen in love with her...an artificial woman preprogrammed to love him. No free will, no options. What she felt for him wasn't real and what he felt for her couldn't be either.

"I leave her in your care. Take her to one of your estates, or whatever. Don't destroy her or sell her—I don't want her harmed in any way. In fact, make sure she's given an identity to make her a free woman. I want her to live to do whatever she wishes...but I never want to see her again."

He left the room without another look.

Chapter Five

℘

Dina was reading when Himla entered the room that had been her home for the past six months. Her home…more like her prison cell, luxurious as it was. In some ways it reminded her of the place where Gall had been held.

In some ways it was, but she could at least leave these walls temporarily. Gall's only restriction as far as she was concerned had been that she not be brought where he could see her, so Himla had taken her everywhere else.

They'd visited many towns and villages, gone to plays and concerts, and he'd even taken her on small trips to other countries on their world, broadening her experiences. That plus the books she read had given her great insight into humanity. She understood many things now. She even occasionally advised Himla on some point of law or the kingdom's politics.

She even understood why Gall had abandoned her. Not that she accepted his reasoning that as a synth she wasn't to be trusted. After long sessions with her designer, Dr. Lassa, she knew far more about who she was.

Despite her origin, she was a woman. Little more—and nothing less.

Himla shook his head at her. "Don't you ever get tired of this?" He indicated the stacks of electronic book disks piled next to the vidscreen, plus the many old-fashioned paper books she'd borrowed from various libraries.

"Not really," she said, but when she shut off the screen she rubbed her eyes wearily. When she looked closely at her reflection in the mirror, she now saw tiny lines in the corners of her eyes. The experience of living marked her face but she didn't mind…she'd rather have those lines than ignorance.

"Wouldn't it be faster to just download what you want to know? You still have the jacks for it."

"Perhaps, but that only really works for facts...to really understand a subject you must go through the process of reading a book the way the author wanted you to. Besides..." she hesitated.

Himla pushed aside a stack of disks and sat on the desk's corner. "Besides it seems more human to do it this way."

Her guardian-captor was too perceptive. "There is that, as well."

"You really want to be human?"

A flash of anger swept through her, something that happened more frequently now. "I *am* human," she snapped at him, "no matter what anyone else thinks."

To her surprise, he smiled. "About time you showed some spunk. You've become a real woman, Dina."

"You didn't believe I was before."

"No," he admitted. "But I didn't really know you, either. Gall said you were, though. At first."

She turned away, hiding her pain. "He changed his mind. He said he never wanted to see me again."

Himla shrugged. "It was a chaotic time. Many things were said then, even by me." He reached out and gently touched her cheek. "Have you given any thought to what I asked?"

She sighed. Yes, Himla did believe her a real woman now. Real enough to fall a little bit in love with, a fine joke given his role in making Gall give her up. He'd asked her to his bed a few days ago but while she enjoyed his company, he wasn't the man she wanted intimacy with.

Dina shook her head. "I care for you, but..."

Himla drew away, disappointed, but she read the understanding in his face. "But you still love him, even now."

She didn't have to answer him. For a while they sat in silence.

"How is he?" Dina hated her need to ask, but Himla had seen him just today.

"He's well. Busy with his position…" he hesitated. "But lonely. He needs someone."

Some of her studies had included the social activities of the crown prince. "There have been many women in his life since he was exonerated." Since he'd abandoned her she left unsaid.

"There has not been the one woman he needs." Himla shook his head. "I'm afraid I have a problem."

Dina turned to him. "Why is that?"

"I swore an oath to obey his orders." He gave a heartfelt sigh. "Trouble is it looks like the best way to be his friend is going to be to break that oath."

* * * * *

Galleanus Ell Vanant stared out the window of his new palace, that of the crown prince of Vanant. How far things had come in six months and yet, not far at all. Yes, he was no longer a prisoner, nor was he in disgrace. He was now heir to the throne, something that he hadn't even anticipated before his brother, in a fit of paranoia, had framed him and then tried to end his life.

Gall shook his head. Apparently Gratus had been worried that the charismatic Gall was too popular with their people and would overshadow him even after he'd taken the throne. He'd taken steps to see to it the brothers would never be compared.

There was no need to worry about that anymore. Their father had not been amused by Gratus conspiring against his younger brother and now Gratus was the one languishing in the luxurious but secure quarters that had been Gall's home for the past few years.

There hadn't been any complaints from the kingdom's people. When Gall had been named crown prince there had been considerable rejoicing on Vanant as Gall wasn't the only person his brother had conspired against over the years.

Dina's testimony had been instrumental in proving his brother's guilt...as a synth she wasn't considered capable of telling a falsehood, consequently she'd been believed. Only a few had heard her speak, but based on her secret testimony Gall had been freed and his brother convicted.

Ironic. He hadn't wanted her near because he didn't trust her, but the court had believed her implicitly.

So now he was free, no longer a prisoner. But in spite of that, one thing from Gall's imprisonment remained. He was still very much alone.

Sure there'd been women since his return. Several women. In fact, as he thought about it, probably too many women. His return to court life and the fact that he no longer suffered from the compulsion that had made his sex life so miserable had led him to many liaisons.

Probably he should have settled with one woman and made her his consort. Certainly his father had made pointed comments about that from time to time. As crown prince he needed an heir and a woman to bear that child.

But no woman appealed to him enough, and after the initial rush of passion, he lost interest in whatever lady he was involved with.

In fact, there'd been no one in his bed for several weeks and he realized he didn't miss sex at all. A fine thing—to have back his ability to make love and not want to take advantage of it.

Not that women didn't still interest him. Lately whenever a small pale-haired woman passed him in a palace hallway he would turn to look, but he was always disappointed when he saw the woman more clearly. He kept searching for hair so pale it was the color of silver, and eyes of golden-brown.

He wouldn't say her name aloud...Dina...but she was whom he wanted, even now. And Dina was lost and he was alone.

"Your highness." It was Himla in the room and the man's presence annoyed him. In the past few months he'd been tempted to ask about Dina, but hadn't dared. He'd told Himla to keep her far from him and much as he wanted to, he couldn't go back on his word now.

"What is it?" he asked, hating the impatience in his voice, but not able to hide it this time. Too many things irritated him these days.

His friend didn't seem to mind. "You haven't been sleeping well."

"So you've decided to keep me company? Or you've brought me some new cure for insomnia?"

"I've brought you something to pass the time."

"A new game? Castles bores me these days. It's been months since I had a worthy opponent."

"No, not a game." Himla seemed to hesitate. "I left it in your room. You can thank me—or not—in the morning." Then he headed for the door.

Curious, Gall opened the door to his suite. At first he didn't see anything, but then a shadow rose from the couch in front of the fireplace, a silhouette against the firelight.

He sucked in a great breath. "Dina?"

She stepped closer, and Gall saw her eyes, a bright blue, and he let his held breath out. Not Dina with her golden eyes. This woman's hair was different too, a darker shade of silver, plus there were other differences…subtle ones.

She smiled, a bright artificial thing, and shook her head. "Who, your highness?"

"You're a pleasuremaid?" he asked, but it wasn't really a question. This wasn't Dina, but he knew she was a synth like her. The slender, voluptuous body, the bone structure, the same perfect skin. She and Dina could have been sisters.

Damn Himla for this. Last thing he needed was a poor copy of what he'd given up.

The woman's smile seemed to sadden but she nodded. "Yes, Prince Galleanus. My name…" she hesitated for a moment. "My name is Lees."

"You're supposed to distract me somehow? I don't need a synth for sex."

She seemed to flinch but her voice remained even. "Of course not, your highness. I'm here to entertain you. Whatever you wish me to do. I can sing, or play an instrument. Or we could play a game."

Her sweet soft voice reminded him of Dina's and for a brief moment he took comfort in that. He was going to tell her to leave, but suddenly her company didn't seem so bad. What could it hurt to have the woman entertain him?

"I don't suppose you play Castles."

Her smile returned and brightened. "Yes, actually, I do."

Trying not to think of the last time he'd matched wits with one her kind, Gall set up the board on an inlaid table and they sat opposite each other in the firelight.

To his surprise Lees turned out to be a worthy opponent. Gall won the first two games, but she made it close to a draw during the second. They were midway through the third game when she moved her cavalry piece in an unusual way. She smiled as he picked up his bowman, then put it down realizing she'd blocked his next move.

Gall stared at the board and her. "How did you know I was going to move there?

"It's what you usually do in that situation…" Lees' voice trailed off and her smile faded. Her hand fluttered up to mouth.

"How did you know that? I've not used that strategy tonight," Gall said. He stared at her, then noticed her fingers, in particular the nails. One was noticeably shorter, bitten nearly to the quick.

"I did make that same move six months ago…with another synth. Another woman," he corrected himself.

Her blue eyes widened. "Your highness..."

Hope rose in him. "Dina. It's you, isn't it?"

This time she didn't deny it. She turned her face, and the firelight danced in her eyes, turning them the familiar gold he remembered and lighting her hair to silver. "Please don't be angry. I know you didn't want me near you."

And he hadn't, and now he couldn't remember why. "But you came to me anyway."

"I...I wanted to see you again."

"I've wanted to see you." He moved around the game table and lifted her to her feet. He stared into her face. "You changed your hair...and your eyes."

"A dye in both. It will fade away."

He stroked her cheek. "I'm glad. I liked them as they were."

She stared at him solemnly. "You liked my hair and eyes...but not me? You said you never wanted to see me again."

"Dina..." he said but he couldn't continue. Explaining how he'd felt then and how he didn't feel that way now was going to take too long.

Instead he kissed her. A long passionate kiss that felt like coming home. Her taste made his cock harden in a way he'd not felt in the six months they'd been apart.

When he drew back a tentative smile took over her face. "Does that mean I can stay?"

"You aren't going anywhere, Dina. Not now."

"You're *demanding* I stay?" Her smile broadened, and he saw a glimpse of a new spirit in her. "But you can't do that. You freed me, remember? I'm not legally even a synth...I have papers to prove it."

"Yes, you are free. But a long time ago I asked you to live by my side and you agreed." Sudden concern ripped through him. "Don't you want to be with me, Dina? Why else would you come here?"

"I came for you. But I want to know it is on my terms that I stay. You sent me away once—I want to be certain you don't do it again."

Gall stilled. "What promises can I make to you?"

"That you agree to let me live by your side."

"You're a synth…"

He wasn't sure why he said it, but it fired a response in her that made him proud. She met his challenge with bright eyes and a firm jaw. "I am a *person*! A woman in love with a man…regardless of how I came to exist."

"You still love me?"

Her anger faded. "Yes. These past six months, I've had a lot of time to think. Dr. Lassa examined me from head to toe. I've somehow become different from the others. How that came to be, I don't know. Dr. Lassa isn't sure, although he thinks it has something to do with the reprogramming, plus the shock I took climbing over the wall. Whatever it was, it changed me. I'm not a simple synth, programmed for one purpose. That used to bother me—that I didn't have a firm purpose, but I've come to terms with it. I know who I am now and I won't be any less than what I can be."

"And what are you?"

"I'm a woman… just that, a thinking, living being. A woman who loves you, Gall. More than that I can't tell you, you'll just have to find out."

He leaned back and stared at her. All the loneliness of the past few months seemed to fade away. For a few days back in his prison, he'd had something precious within his grasp. A companion—someone to share his life with. What did it matter whether or not she'd been born in the normal way? All that was important was that she existed.

She wasn't completely human…but she wasn't anything else, either. She was capable of love and she loved him.

And he realized he loved her, too and for the first time in six months, he didn't feel alone. "Stay with me, Dina. I need you."

She relaxed in his arms and he saw her smile, a real smile this time, not the artificial one she'd put on while pretending to be Lees. "I need you, too. That's why I'm here."

Barely able to control his joy, Gall lifted her in his arms. She was still a small woman, curved in all the right places. He carried her to the bed that had been his alone for too long. Now he would share it with her. Now he'd share everything with her.

Her clothes ended up on the floor as fast as he could pull them off. He wanted to be slow but somehow couldn't take the time. Long weeks of deprivation, long months of loneliness had caught up with him. Now Gall wanted her skin perfectly bare next to his.

Dina seemed no better. Her hands pulled his shirt so hard that fasteners flew across the room. "I'll fix that later," she told him when he startled. "Now I need you naked."

He pulled off his own pants and boots, sparing their fastenings. And then he was in bed with her, and they were entwined together. He kissed her, tilting her head to angle his mouth against him.

Again it was like coming home, her kiss, the familiarity, the passion. She opened to him and he swept his tongue deep inside. "Mine, Dina. You are mine."

"I am my own. But you can have me."

He worked his way down her body, kissing and licking, until he was poised just outside her pussy, the warmth and scent of her enticing him. He'd been inside her many times, but hadn't finished there. She'd cured him of his compulsion but had yet to reap the benefit of it.

Gall smiled to himself. Tonight he'd rectify that.

He leaned in for an intimate kiss and she moaned, hips lifting to his mouth. So responsive…her arousal flooded his tongue and he felt like climaxing on the spot. How had he gone so long without her taste? He bore down on her, pulling her clit into his mouth and suckled it gently. Dina moaned again, and her hands clutched his hair.

"So good…"

Good? He was just getting started!

Gall set to work and by the time he finished, Dina was nearly inarticulate. Moans had developed into cries and then screams. She lay limp when he finally rose up over her. "Dina, it's time we made love properly. I want to come inside you."

She stilled. "I need to get up for a moment."

Confused, he stared at her. "What is it?"

She smiled. "I'm sorry…I should have done it earlier, but I wasn't sure… I'm past due for a contraceptive shot. I haven't been with anyone so there was no need. I have a barrier, though. I just need to put it in."

A barrier was a thin film to prevent conception that a woman slid inside her vagina. That Dina hadn't already put one in told him how uncertain she'd been of her reception from him.

He didn't let her up. "You can have children?"

"Of course, Gall. I'm no different that way than any other woman. Pleasuremaids are given shots to prevent them conceiving, but they can if their master wishes them to."

He hadn't thought of that. Dina was fertile—and the woman he desired above all others. And as crown prince there was something he needed to solidify his position.

She rose to head for the lavatory, but he caught her arm. "No, Dina. Don't put it in."

"I have to, Gall."

"You don't."

She stared at him with those odd blue eyes of hers and he wished they were already back to the golden brown color he loved.

"Gall, you are crown prince now. Only your consort is allowed to have your children."

"So become my consort, Dina."

She stared at him with wide eyes. "You're the crown prince of Vanant. You can't make me your consort."

"Why not?"

"I'm a synth, a pleasuremaid!" she cried. "No one would ever accept it."

"Who says that's what you are? You are one of a kind, Dina. There are no others like you anywhere and only a few know what you were." He used the past tense deliberately. She was no more a pleasuremaid now than his brother was crown prince. The latter had proved unworthy of his position, Dina was worthy of much more.

"I want to marry you, Dina, and keep you with me always. That's what you asked me for. And I want no other woman to bear my children."

She seemed stricken. "But Gall. Suppose someone does find out. The king could disinherit you."

Gall laughed. "I've been disinherited before, Dina. Having you with me made it bearable. Not having you has made the last six months nearly intolerable. Given the choice I'd rather have you than be on my father's throne."

He pressed closer to her, pushing her back onto the bed. Parting her knees he moved between them and poised just outside her pussy.

"Don't put anything between us, Dina. You say you are a person. I know you are the woman I want to make love to, and if you bear my child, that's all to the good. Do you want my baby?"

Her hands cupped his face. "I would love it. But, Gall, you are certain this is what you want?"

He smiled and entered her with one swift thrust that wrung a moan out of her and a short groan from him. He set up a fast pace that made her cry out in pleasure over and over again, until she shuddered beneath him, her hands clutching at his back.

As she climaxed, her shaft tightened around his cock, milking it, but Gall held on for just a moment longer. Leaning over her he stared into her eyes, letting her see all the love he held for her. "I've never been so certain of anything in my life."

And then he let passion override him and he emptied himself into her. His seed shot deep into his woman, hopefully to begin a new life, a baby made from both of them. A baby for them to love—a child to be raised to be tolerant of others, no matter how they came to exist.

Of course it was possible that she wouldn't conceive this time, but as Gall collapsed next to her, and drew his new consort into his arms, he decided not to let that bother him.

If it didn't happen tonight, they'd just have to do it again.

The End

Also by Cricket Starr

ঙ

Divine Interventions 1: Violet Among the Roses

Divine Interventions 2: Echo In the Hall

Divine Interventions 3: Nemesis of the Garden

Ellora's Cavemen: Legendary Tails I (*anthology*)

Hollywood After Dark: Fangs for the Memories

Hollywood After Dark: Ghosts of Christmas Past

Holiday Reflections (*anthology*)

Memories To Come

The Doll

Two Men and a Lady (*anthology*)

If you are a fan of Cricket's Hollywood After Dark vampire stories, be sure to see the first in the series, *All Night Inn*, at Cerridwen Press (www.cerridwenpress.com), written under the name Janet Miller.

About the Author

Cricket Starr lives in the San Francisco Bay area with her husband of more years than she chooses to count. She loves fantasies, particularly sexual fantasies, and sees her writing as an opportunity to test boundaries. Her driving ambition is to have more fun than anyone should or could have. While published in other venues under her own name, she's found a home for her erotica writing here at Ellora's Cave.

Cricket welcomes comments from readers. You can find her website and email address on her author bio page at www.ellorascave.com.

TEMPT ME TWICE

Renee Luke

Chapter One
Working the Seduction

ജ

Latoya stared at her husband's broad back, his well-defined muscles swathed in smooth dark skin. The color of rich chocolate and just as tempting. She blinked. Twice. The sting of tears burned behind her eyes and tightened her throat. Her gaze slid down his spine to where the shadows of the sheet draped over his hip obscured his rounded ass and corded thighs.

As fine as it was, it was still his back. Across a cool span of Egyptian cotton sheets. On his side of the bed. She longed to reach for him. To touch the silken texture of his flesh.

To be welcomed.

But he presented his back to her when not so long ago she would have been tucked into his embrace. Secured in his arms. Fitted to his body.

Swiping a lone tear from her cheek, Latoya inhaled. *A mistake.* The masculine scent of him, mingling with the faint hint of cologne prompted her body's response. Liquid heat seeped to her panties. Her nipples beaded with need.

If only she knew Dante wouldn't spurn her advance, she'd close the distance between them and demand he made love to her with his thick length of cock.

She licked her lips and closed her eyes to ward off a rising moan. The ring around her finger should've been all the permission she needed.

But she knew better. His back meant leave him alone. They hardly spoke at all, let alone made love anymore. She couldn't have her husband when she wanted. Not with this invisible wedge between them.

Hell, how had another tear escaped? she wondered, dabbing the moisture from her lips. Lips that longed for her husband's kisses. His love. Affection.

And as aroused as she was, she wasn't foolish enough to deny it. She longed for *sex*.

Rolling to her other side, Latoya fluffed her pillow and ignored the desire pouring through her system. She had to focus on a bigger problem — lure Dante back between her thighs and into her heart.

Or divorce him.

* * * * *

Sex didn't fix everything. Latoya knew that. But it was a damned good icebreaker. A good way to melt away tension. And the tool she planned on implementing to ease the strain between her and Dante. At least for now.

Closing her eyes, she imagined the last time she and her husband had been intimate. Their nightly lovemaking had slipped to a couple of times a week, then less. Days would go by. Weeks. Oftentimes the only physical touches she'd get from him were when he worked her with his morning wood. Though a nice way to start the day, it didn't do much for her. Certainly wasn't the sort of quickie that got her off. But she enjoyed the emotional part of his easing the rocked-up erection he began each day with.

Then his workload had increased and he started leaving the house earlier in the morning. He'd slip from bed before the sun rose and be gone from the house before she roused from sleep. Those morning fucks just took too long.

Or maybe he just isn't attracted to me anymore, she thought, swallowing sorrow past the tightness of her throat.

Opening her eyes, she fiddled with her sundress. A built-in bra? She rolled her eyes, hoping her tits wouldn't pop out the top. She smoothed the cream-colored rayon, liking the way it set off her dark skin that glittered with scented lotion.

Turning her attention to the door of her husband's office, she read the nameplate—*Dante Ross, Chief Financial Officer*.

Brushing her fingertips across his name, Latoya recalled how they'd met four years ago. At a gas station, when her ATM card was eaten by the machine and she'd had no cash. A fine-ass man had come to the rescue. Filled her tank, then jotted his number on the back of the receipt. When she'd promised to pay him back, he'd stolen a kiss and said it was all the payment he'd need.

And the romance had begun with nightly phone calls. While they'd talk, she'd silently doodle her name with his—*Latoya Ross*. He was the kind of brothah who was serious about his shit. He proposed on his knee eight months into the courtship. They married seven months later.

And now divorce papers were hidden in the trunk of her car. Not that she wanted to use them. She hoped to God she didn't have to. They were a worse-case scenario. Preparations for what happened if she couldn't interest him again. Or worse, if someone else had.

Dante was *her* man. Unless he'd already strayed, she meant to see that he didn't.

Taking a deep breath, she strolled into his office, closing the door behind her with one hand.

He glanced up as the wood clunked into its frame. "Toya, what are you doing here?" he asked, concern lacing the deep timbre of his voice.

She smiled, sliding her hand down to the lock and secured it with a twist. "I brought you lunch." She lifted the square, white box that contained a hot steak sandwich and fries. Walking to his desk, she swayed her hips, licked her lips and kept her gaze locked on her man's.

"You're off work today?"

"I took it off."

"Why?"

Biting her bottom lip, she thought over how much to tell

him. *Showing* him would work best, she decided, fighting back a grin. "To do this for you."

Dante stared at his wife. She hadn't done much for him recently. *So what's up?* he wondered, watching her delicious round ass as she strolled around his office, twisting closed the blinds on both of his windows. Each spin of the privacy verticals drained thought from his head as blood poured to his cock.

He shifted in his seat, making room in his slacks as he thickened, watching the sensual sway of her movements. Smooth and slender legs that dropped a mile to the floor from beneath her way-too-short dress. Cleavage that begged to be licked. And, knowing damned well they didn't need privacy to eat—he flipped open the box she'd brought—a sandwich and potatoes.

He cleared his throat, lust making it go dry. "You took the day off to bring me food?"

"Shhh…" she whispered, moving across the space. Leaning over his desk, she pressed her fingertips to his lips. She moved around the tabletop between them and eased in front of him, pushing him back in his rolling leather office chair.

"Toya?" he said, lifting a brow. The scent of her sweet feminine skin and floral lotion overpowered his senses.

"Shhh…" she whispered again, lowering before him. "No, Daddy, I took off work to give you this." She licked her full bottom lip and gave a little whimper as she scraped her nails down his chest, flicking over his nipple beneath the material of his button-up shirt.

An aching throb started in his dick. Groaning, Dante watched his wife's eyes. They sparkled with mischief and were hooded with arousal, locked on his belt and zipper fly. He gulped down a breath, then slid a glance at his windows to make sure they were closed all the way.

Oh, hell, yeah, she was up to something…and he was damned well going to enjoy it.

Leaning back, he adjusted his body, giving her fuller access to his hard-on, and hoped she'd hurry the fuck up before he blew his wad in his boxer shorts. Seemingly in tune with his urgency, she slid the leather from his belt buckle and yanked open the single metal tooth holding it in place.

With a twist of her wrist, she opened the top button on his pants. He reached for her, brushing a knuckle against her cheek, splaying his fingers across her sleek hair. It wasn't easy to keep from sliding his hand behind her neck and yanking her mouth down to his cock, but he managed somehow to allow her to set the pace. Too damn slow, he inwardly growled.

"You relax, Daddy." She pressed a hand to his abdomen and pushed him back in his chair. "Enjoy your lunch break," she said softly as she tugged down the zipper of his pants, then used both hands to widen the gap by pushing the material over his hips.

Dante groaned, reclining in his seat as he caressed the line of her jaw. The slope of her throat. The wild pulse racing in rhythm with his. God, he missed touching her this way. Feeling her body respond to his. Seeing the longing in her dark, clear eyes.

Talented fingers crept beneath his boxers, sliding the elastic lower and setting him free. His cock sprang up, throbbing against her palms as she cupped his balls with one hand and wrapped slender fingers around his shaft with the other.

"You're so big, Daddy. Are you happy to see me?" She stroked upward, running her thumb over his head, swirling in the bead of pre-cum. She used it for lubricant as she tightened her hold, and rubbed downward again.

He pumped his hips. Twice. Orgasm already building deep in his gut. "Yeah, baby, I'm happy to see you," he said, closing his eyes, then gritting his teeth for control.

Her mouth closed around his head. Wet. Silken. Sultry.

"Daaaammmmmn, girl," Dante hissed, his eyes popping open to see the back of his wife's head as she took him in. Gripping the armrests, his body tensed, wanting to prolong this, but it'd been a long time since he'd been sexed. He feared it wouldn't take much to bring him to a quick climax.

She took him deeper, the tight passage of her mouth hot against his flesh. Her tongue swirled around him, working the pulsing vein that ran down the underside of his cock.

He was too long and thick for his petite wife to deep-throat him, but hell, she knew how to compensate. Fingers encased the few inches her lips couldn't, and massaged his erection with caresses that mimicked the tempo of her mouth.

Up... Down... Up... Down...

Breaths came quickly, burning in his lungs.

Every muscle in his body taut, he focused on the heat swirling around his dick, the slickness of her saliva, the breathy whimpers that sent spiraling emotion coursing though his blood. He studied the shadows her eyelashes cast on her cheeks. The tendrils of hair that escaped the smoothed-back bun she'd tied at the nape of her neck. Firm breasts and coffee-colored pert nipples that peeked over the top of her dress. The lushness of her damp lips as she took his dick deeper. And faster.

Working him.

His nuts drew up tight. Orgasm building now, like a stone gathers momentum as it rolls down a slope. "Baby," he growled, his hands tight against the leather armrests. "Slow down, baby."

Latoya moaned as she shook her head slightly. No way was she slowing down. She couldn't get enough of the solid feel of him pressed against her tongue. Shoved down her throat. She couldn't get enough of the masculine salty taste, the bittersweetness of looming fulfillment. Lapping her tongue against his raging pulse, she felt him tense. Heard the way he sucked air between his teeth, could feel his legs trembling beneath her forearms.

And knew he was going to come.

Wanting to see the orgasm claim his features, she slanted back and lifted her gaze to his face, not pulling back from the rapid pace of her lips around his dick. His lids drooped half closed. Beads of sweat glistened on his brown skin. Nostrils flared. Tension throbbed at his temples. Tightened his jaw.

Closing her fingers against his hard-on, she felt the swell of cum beneath her palm. It surged up his shaft. His hips bucked under her. A raspy groan tore from his lips, a cry so raw it seized her heart with love.

"Toya—"

Hot liquid filled her cheeks. Shot down her throat, his erection pulsating. Dante's body shook violently, thrusting his hips upward as he emptied his sticky seed onto her tongue. Licking up every last drop of the pearly cream, she slowly eased his wrung cock from between her lips. And was unable to contain her grin of satisfaction as she sat back on her heels and gazed at the serenity and awe on her husband's face.

He sat there, completely tranquil, the jagged pants of his breathing slowly returning to a steady rate. Clothing disheveled, lunch getting cold, and her panties soaking wet with arousal, Latoya glanced at his dick and thought about pulling up her skirt, shoving her panties aside and climbing on. Resting against the cotton boxer-shorts, his depleted erection told her he needed a little time.

Though she wanted him inside her—badly—the contentment of getting him off was unbelievably satisfying. Oh, yeah, she wanted to fuck, she thought, licking her lips. That yummy cock of his, she wanted it rocked-up, so hard it was throbbing. But after blowing a nut as big as the one he'd just blasted down her throat, it could take him a while to recuperate.

She could wait.

Until tonight. Besides, this was about getting her man interested again. About salvaging a marriage that meant everything to her.

"Quit your job." His voice was low, raspy.

"Huh?" Latoya stood, shifting her hips to allow the material of her dress to fall correctly on her body and pulling up the top to conceal her nipples. Little support the built-in had offered.

"Quit your job, girl." He adjusted his dick, pulling up his boxers and shifting his hips as he righted his slacks. He was grinning wide as he zippered up. The ends of his leather belt hung loose and he made no move to secure it.

Latoya bit her lip, unsure if she should take him seriously or not. "Why?"

He stood. Mere inches separated their bodies, but she could feel his heat. Smell the cologne he'd splashed on that morning. See the bulge in his pants begin to grow. Taking a breath, she tilted back her head and looked into his eyes. He was looking down at her, unspoken words lingering on his lips. Whatever he'd wanted to say remained unsaid.

The intense look in his midnight stare startled her. Unreadable, she couldn't tell if he was angry and brooding or if desire was again building. His warm palm settled on her hip and she swayed into him.

And he chuckled. "So you can bring me lunch all the time." He bent and kissed her cheek, then reached behind her to the box of food she'd brought as a rouse. "Thanks, baby." He opened the box and lifted the cold sandwich. "You want to share it with me?" But he didn't wait for a reply before he bit into the tepid steak.

What the fuck? She gives him a damned good blowjob and he gives her the casual brush-off? Shaking her head, Latoya moved away from her husband, feeling a little disappointed that he didn't want to talk about things. But a little quick head wasn't all that impressive or persuasive enough to open up his heart. Not after many cold, lonely nights.

Besides, this was just the beginning of the seduction she's planned for her man.

"You enjoy it, Daddy." She licked her lips and winked at him. "I ate already."

He laughed.

Moving to the door, she turned the lock, then glanced over

her shoulder. "You won't be late, will you?"

He shook his head.

Smiling, Latoya went out the door. She had preparations to make for later that required a visit to her favorite lingerie boutique.

* * * * *

Dante stared at the ceiling. Flat on his back with his head resting on his hands folded behind him, he tried to ignore the sounds of his wife in the bathroom just beyond the giant four-poster bed. His cock wasn't having as easy a time ignoring her, though. He glanced down to where the sheets were forming a nine-inch tent.

Drawing in a ragged breath, his thoughts skittered back to the kick-ass head-job she'd surprised him with earlier at the office. His pulse ticked at his temples. Though he wanted her — bad — it was fear that had his heart racing, not lust.

Something was wrong, he just couldn't figure out what.

Closing his eyes, Dante remembered events over the last several months. She'd totally pulled away from him, barely acknowledging him when he got home from a day of work, rarely fixing dinner, ambivalent or unconcerned about his needs. Too tired from her job, she often rebuffed making love at night and after a while, even their morning bouts of sex seemed like a chore to her.

Until he'd extended his workday so he could slip out without bothering her. Intimacy came to a damned screeching halt. But not from lack of desire. He wanted his wife so badly, he could feel the lust stir in his gut. Desire seeped all the way to his bones. He wanted her happy, too, and if that meant a little space and no sex, then hell, he was trying his best to respect it.

Until she'd torn down the non-contact wall with skillful hands and a talented tongue.

What was going on with her?

In addition to lunch and a damn good sucking, tonight she'd fixed his favorite meal. Chicken fried steaks. Mashed potatoes, not from a box. Corn on the cob slathered in butter. Hell, she'd lit candles and had Jodeci softly pulsing from the speakers. Lights doused. She'd even opened a bottle of wine, though sipped very little.

Thoughtful things she'd done for him a year ago. Wouldn't have even been suspicious six months ago. But out of the blue? After a cold spell?

Opening his eyes, he turned to look at the closed bathroom door. When he'd finished cleaning up the dinner dishes, he'd gone to the bathroom and found her birth-control pills. Counting the tiny pink and green tablets, it appeared they were being taken.

She couldn't be pregnant. Could she? His throat tightened, unsure how he felt about that. She was keeping something from him.

Goddammit, she better not be fucking around on him! His hands fisted into the pillowcase behind him. Tension tore through his body, each muscle tightening with a fierce possessiveness. A growl erupted from his lips, anger burning fire in his lungs.

Closing his eyes, he struggled to calm the erratic breaths, the rhythm of his heart. Was that was all the tenderness was about? So he wouldn't suspect she was screwing someone else? Did she think home-cooked meals and dick-sucking lips would throw him off the scent of disloyalty? Could his once loving wife have stooped so low?

"Hi, Daddy." Her sweet voice sounded from the doorway.

Opening his eyes, he turned toward her. She was dressed in the sexiest little strips of satin and lace he'd ever seen. Gulping, his gaze fixed on the minute pale cloth covering her luscious body. Pink lace cupped the under-swell of her tits, so transparent he could see the dark circles of her areolas. See how her nipples puckered.

His mouth watered.

Anger awash with passion.

She put her hands out to her sides, then spun showing him her backside. "You like?"

Hell, yeah, he liked. Matching pink lace slid between the round globes of her full ass. The thong panties were secured on the sides by rosettes of white satin ribbon. Roses he'd like to tear off with his teeth.

Brown, freshly shaved skin shimmered down legs he wanted to wrap around him. Across thighs he wanted to get between. Her hair was loose, the tight curls falling around her face, a combination of girlishly sweet and wildly untamed.

Coming up on one elbow, he lifted the sheet and arched an eyebrow. Her gaze dropped to his rock-hard dick. "You look gooood."

She laughed, then turned back toward him and came to the side of the bed. "Did you have a nice lunch today?" she asked, her lush lips tipped into a smile.

Teasing was dangerous. His cock bucked at her words. Pre-cum seeped onto his head. She was deliberately trying to incite him. "It was all right," he taunted back, shrugging his shoulders. He strained to keep the smile from his face.

Dark eyes popped open, then narrowed on his face. After a silent moment, she answered his shrug with one of her own, and plopped down next to him on the pillows. The floral scent of her lotion wafted in the air. A sigh escaped parted lips. "I guess next time I'll have to be faster so the food doesn't get cold."

Faster? He about choked. He'd come in record speed. His sac drew up in memory.

With his gaze fixed on her, he watched as her eyes caressed his naked flesh, lingering on his hard-on. She licked her lips, emitting a breathy moan.

Latoya Ross was the most alluring woman he'd ever met.

And she was *his* wife.

He would please her. Kiss her. Lick her. *He'd* be the one easing his dick into the tight, wet heat of her pussy.

His wife.

He'd make her remember that.

"Come here, Toya," he said in gruff voice. Putting his hand around her waist, he dragged her closer to him, then crushed his mouth down on hers.

Latoya gasped, startled by the demand in his kiss. This wasn't about tenderness, but about possession. Opening her mouth, she gave over to the kiss. It was more than she'd had in weeks and the feeling of closeness was irresistible. Exactly what she needed.

With his hands roving across her body, he slanted his head, his tongue sweeping past her teeth. Delving in her mouth. He tasted masculine and heady. Fresh like toothpaste. He slid his tongue against hers. Nipped at her bottom lip with his teeth. Commanded a response.

Strong fingers closed around one breast, his thumb grating across her nipple. Latoya moaned, the texture of lace setting flame to her skin. Arousal seeped onto her inner thighs, swelled her clit. She squeezed her legs together, hoping for a reprieve, but was met instead by the pressure of her panties.

Turning on her side, she leaned into her husband, rotating her hips against the length of his erection. The contact both offered relief and spurred the tightening hunger.

She settled her hand on his upper arm, the muscles bulging. His chocolate skin was damp. Her fingertips grazed across his corded shoulders. Skimmed over his back. Tightening on his firm ass, she pulled him toward her as she rotated her hips into him. Breaking the kiss, she gasped for air, then whispered against his mouth. "Please, Daddy."

"You want *me*, Toya?" He flipped her onto her back, his mouth landing on the swell of her breast above the lace. A hand smoothed down her belly. Fingers dipped beneath satin rosebuds. Inched forward. "You want me?"

"Yessss…"

He parted her pussy with his fingers, twirling in the slickness. He dipped in knuckle deep, thrusting into her with one finger, then adding a second. Her legs fell apart. "Is this what you want, baby?" he asked, flicking his tongue across the bead of her nipple, then scraping it with his teeth.

Latoya moaned and lolled her head to the side, closing her eyes.

"Or this?" He thrust his fingers deeper, then curled them forward against her G-spot. She trembled, but he didn't relent. He found her clit with his thumb and circled, as he mimicked the motion of fucking with his hand.

"Yessss…" she hissed, her back arching off the bed. Blindly reaching for his cock, she sighed as her fingers closed around him. He pulsed against her palm. "This, Daddy. Give me this."

She was rolling her hips into each movement of his hand. Whimpering with each press of his thumb against her clit. The build was there. The spiraling tightness of impending orgasm. Tremors cascaded over her body. Dante sucked her nipple into the hot depth of his mouth, laving it with his tongue.

Muscles clamped down, pleasure humming in her blood. Crying out, "Dante!" She came. Hard. Shivers quivering inside her pussy, tingling her clit, tightening around her husband's hand. Emotion tightened her throat. "Dante," she whispered, turning her head toward his chest, tears welling behind her eyes.

But her man gave her no time to wallow in sentiment. He knelt between her thighs. Grabbing her hips, he took the rosebuds in his hand, slid the panties down her legs, flinging them away before he draped her legs over his muscular ass.

His name from her lips…that's what he'd wanted to hear.

A satisfied smile claimed him. Taking his dick in his hand, Dante positioned his head against her tight, juicy pussy. Teased her lips with the end of his throbbing flesh. Used her cum to lubricate his entry. She moaned, lifting her hips and rotating her ass, but he gave her just an inch. He tightened his jaw, restraint dissipating.

"Daddy, please," Toya sobbed, reaching for him, clawing at his arms. The spill of light from the open bathroom doorway reflected a shimmering of sweat across her ripe body. "Plea...se..."

Yeah, beg.

This was *his* pussy. He'd fuck it when he was ready. As hard and as fast as he wanted.

He slammed into her, filling her tight, wet heat with all his nine inches.

She arched off the bed, a cry wrenched from her damp, parted lips. "Aahhhh."

Grinding his hips, he pulled out, then drove into her again. "This is mine," he growled through clenched teeth. "Is it mine?"

Toya was writhing now, rolling her hips upward, curving her back to accept him. Her mouth parted, breathing shallow pants. Her black loose curls looked wild against his sheets. "Mm...ahh...yours...Daddy."

Powerful and steady, Dante settled into a vigorous rhythm of fucking his wife. Curling one of her legs behind him, he draped the other over his shoulder, running his tongue along the smooth skin just above her knee, nipping his teeth against her skin. Spurred on by her cries. Her moans. By the way she responded to him. By the way she not only welcomed his dick, but how passionately she was screwing him back.

Changing the angle, Toya pushed up, one hand splayed across the bed behind her. The other reached for him. Cum filled the base of his cock. Groaning, he held the rush back, her tight cunt making restraint damned hard. His balls were tight as they were slammed against her sopping wet pussy.

He swallowed hard, keeping his jaw tight and hips pumping. The sight of his wife's lush body shaking with the force of his hard-on and thrusting tore at the remaining shards of his control. He closed his eyes, wanting desperately to prolong being encased in her heat before he lost it and came. But it'd been so long. And she was hot. Tight. Wet.

Toya's leg slipped from his shoulder, down his arm, then curled behind him. Her heel settled on the back of his thigh. Pressed. Urged him faster. Deeper.

Leaning forward, Latoya curved her fingers around her man's neck and dragged him closer. She nuzzled her face into the arc of his throat, ran her tongue across his salty sweat-covered delicious chocolate skin. Lips nipped on the fleshy part of his ear. Kissed along the straight line of his jaw. Sucked his lower lip into her mouth. He moaned into her, his body jerking, then going taut. His hand settled firmly on her hips, holding her still as he struggled for breath. "Not yet, baby."

No, not yet. First she wanted to be kissed. Fitting her mouth on his, she eased her tongue past his full lips. Met his. Led him back. Emotion coursed through her body. This was the physical connection she'd been missing with her man. They parted, took a breath, then kissed again. Deep, tender, enthralling.

This was the intimacy she longed for from her husband. Opening her thighs wider, she drew up her knees and pressed her tits against his chest. He thrust in, grinding into her clit. Tremors started in her toes. Heat spread over her skin. All nine inches throbbed, rigid right where she needed him.

Orgasm burst. "Dante!"

The muscles on his shoulders bunched. His legs shook. His body went taut, then jerked hard into her, as his eyes rolled slightly back. Through gritted teeth, he said against her mouth, "This is...my pussy..."

She could feel him pulse deep inside her as a wad of cum sped from his balls, up his dick and filled her cunt. Sticky. Shudders overpowered his body, until every muscle went slack and he collapsed on top of her, supporting the brunt of his weight on his forearms.

Their bodies cooled. Breathing slowed. Minutes ticked by before Dante eased from her body and rolled to his side. His breathing was deep and even, his lashes resting against his cheeks. "Come here, girl," he whispered, pulling her against his naked body.

And then he slept.

Snuggling into his heat, Latoya closed her eyes and inhaled the earthiness of sex. Subtle hints of Obsession lingered on his skin. Climax perfumed the sweat-dampened sheets. Dismissing the idea of shedding her bra for comfort, she drew closer. No way was she leaving her man's arms. This is exactly where she wanted to be.

Swallowing down the tightness in her throat, she'd not think about all the things that were left unsaid. All the things that still needed to be fixed between them. But at least he wasn't on his side of the bed. At least tonight she was secure in his embrace, fitted against him. Their marriage still needed work, but one step at a time.

With a sigh, Latoya fell into a sated sleep.

Chapter Two
Keeping It Real

ॐ

Some things had changed. Some had not.

Dante stared down at Toya as she slept, her lush lips slightly parted, her long lashes castings shadows on her smooth, brown cheeks. She sighed, then smiled, instinctively reaching toward his side of the bed. Where he longed to be. His throat constricted. Tightness seized his chest.

Oh, God, he loved his wife. Taking an unsteady breath, he bent and kissed her cheek, lingering long enough so he could smell the sweetness of her skin, feel the warmth of her sighs, hear her whisper his name.

Glancing at his watch, he knew he had to leave. But hell, he didn't want to. He wanted to strip off his suit and climb naked into bed with her again. To take her into his arms and show her how much he loved her. Show her the best way he knew how — by making love. All the coldness of the last months seemed to have melted away and she was all fiery heat. But there were moments when he'd see trouble in the caramel of her eyes. Uncertainty. He knew deep down to his soul that she was still holding something back.

Rubbing the building tension in his neck, he rolled his shoulders, wishing he knew what to do to make things right. Letting the air hiss between his teeth, Dante grabbed his keys and cell from the dresser and headed out the door, leaving his beautiful wife to sleep.

Tugging the blanket to her chin, Latoya wafted in contented half-sleep. She could hear her husband's car start and the garage door slide open. Grabbing his pillow, cooling from his body heat, she settled the cotton over her face, shielding out dawn as light seeped between the slots of the mini-blinds.

Stretching, she could feel their cum slick on her sore inner thighs. This morning he'd awakened her with his rocked-up dick, then fucked the shit out of her doggie-style. Though, at the very end he'd been thoughtful enough to reach around her and work her clit right before he spurted his nut.

She'd been taking care of his morning wood for the last ten days, and sexing him good each night when the day would end and they'd climb into bed.

But nothing had been said. They still didn't talk. His hours were longer than hers. He always left the house first and returned later. Shrugging out of his work clothes, he'd change into shorts and a T-shirt, then lounge on the sofa in front of the TV.

They'd eat dinner making casual conversation, then curl up together and watch a movie or a few shows. Didn't make communication easy.

The tension was no longer palpable, but nothing was solved. Yeah, things were better, but unless they discussed the issues — what had gotten between them in the first place — it was liable to happen again.

Frustrated, she swiped away a few tears. Fear spun through her dreams. Yeah, they'd been making love again. The sex between them was impassioned, loving, sometimes ardent, sometimes tender. But it was just sex. A strangled sob escaped her lips. What if it was the only thing her husband wanted from her? The only thing they had in common anymore? What if it was all there could be between them, when she longed so deeply for their friendship?

She skimmed the skin above her breast with her fingertips, feeling the lingering sting of the hickey he'd given her just over her heart. With a sigh, she turned on her side, cocooning into the bed, and was lulled by its warmth back to sleep.

* * * * *

Off work at noon, Latoya smiled as she ran errands, first stopping by the cleaners, back to her favorite lingerie boutique, then the grocery store. Biting her bottom lip, she recalled how little work she'd done that morning, instead cruising the net for relationship books and enticing dinner recipes.

She'd found both. Online, she'd skimmed excerpts of five different books, a few of the passages hitting close enough to home that liquid filled her eyes and she struggled to breathe. But mixed with symptoms, real solutions were offered and suggested. Feeling excited about the opportunity to improve their marriage, she'd ordered two, then searched through some recipes for the perfect dinner.

Downloaded and printed, she grinned at her purse as she pushed the wobbly-wheeled cart toward the seafood section, intent on getting shrimp big enough to butterfly and two king crab legs. Wanting their evening to be perfect, she even planned on going through the trouble of clarifying the butter, before dipping steaming crab meat in.

Tonight she'd welcome him home. Take care of all his needs by filling his stomach then working an orgasm from his cock. Leave him wrung and sated.

And then she'd get him to talk to her.

Dragging in a deep breath, she ignored the apprehension coiling in her gut. Things between them had been so good for the last week and a half she didn't want to risk stirring things up by saying the truths between them and facing their problems head-on. But without putting their issues behind them, the lack of communication would haunt every aspect of their relationship.

Though divorce papers remained hidden in her trunk, she didn't want to use them. Didn't want to end up being part of the statistics that claimed black couples don't stay married. She loved Dante too much to lose him, but she couldn't imagine years of tension and walking on eggshells either. Didn't want to allow her mind to wonder about his faithfulness, because if she wasn't on the receiving end of his affection and attention, maybe there was another sistah.

Shrugging off the painful worry, she focused on the positive. The plan to lure her husband back between her legs had worked. Just thinking of the way he'd been working her made her panties wet. Her nipples harden. Arousal set her body on fire, the memory of his love making so real she moaned.

"You all right?" an older woman asked, standing behind her in line.

Heat flamed across her cheeks. "Oh, yeah." She slanted her head toward the seafood display case. "Just thinking about dinner."

"I hear that. Damn good price for shrimps that size."

Latoya nodded, smiling.

"You planning something special? Wine, shrimp, sweet-cream butter."

Oh, yeah, she was arranging something special. Not just dinner, but an entire night. An evening which could possibly make or break her marriage. She took a deep breath. "Dinner for my husband." Turning her attention to the attendant, she placed her order.

"Isn't that nice."

She smiled, knowing the comment didn't warrant a reply. A few silent moments passed, then she collected her items as they were handed to her. "Thanks."

"You have a good night, now, you hear," the woman said as Latoya turned to leave.

"Oh, I will." She winked, then walked away, the sound of the woman's laughter fading in the background. Oh, lawdy, she hoped the night went well.

* * * * *

Dante gripped his steering wheel, the garage dark around him. Closing his eyes, he swallowed down the bitterness of bile rising from his gut. After the last ten days, he thought things

spreading her thighs and binding her legs around him. Blue eyelet bunched at her hips. Dante slapped his palm harshly against her naked ass, sliding his fingers back over the smooth skin to the narrow strip of cloth that dipped between her cheeks. He wound his fingers in the thin T-back panties.

And yanked, tearing the delicate material. She caught her breath, then sighed into his mouth as matching eyelet fell to the floor. Their lips pressed together, Dante thrust his tongue into her mouth in the same furious rhythm he wanted to fuck. Breathing heavy, his fingertips grazed over her butt, forward, then dipped to the middle of her spread thighs.

And found her pussy sopping wet. Aroused. So ready for him. His body shook. A fiery ball of cum throbbed in his dick, ready to explode. He fought back his orgasm, needing to get inside her.

Needing her to feel every solid inch of what she'd be missing.

Holding his wife against the wall with the weight of his body, Dante used his free hand to shove down his clothing. The belt clanked as the expensive slacks dropped around his ankles. Jostling with his boxers, he pushed the cotton just far enough down to be out of the way, then took his rocked-up cock in his hand. An erratic pulse throbbed against his palm.

He guided his swollen head to where slick liquid poured from his wife's cunt, his knees damned near buckling. Putting a hand on each hip, he drove into her. Hard. She cried out against his lips, her back arching off the wall. A picture frame crashed to the floor, the glass shattering.

Ahhh…she was so tight around him. Incredibly hot. Slamming into her again, the wall rattled. Trinkets in the china cabinet fell, breaking to bits.

Frenzied now, he thrust into his wife, sweat beads rolled from his brow. Again. Out. In again. Until his sac smacked against her.

Bending his knees, he drove upward, plunging his cock into the pussy he'd married three years ago.

A chill broke out across his body. The tremors began, as the building climax overcame him. Hot cum erupted, his body jerking violently. His eyes rolled. His head fell back. A raspy roar was wrenched from deep in his lungs.

Using every ounce of self-control he possessed, he pulled from her lush body, wanting to deprive her of feeling the shudders of his orgasm. Of the satisfaction her tight pussy had granted him. Wrapping a hand around the base of his shaft, he finished the job with two quick strokes.

Droplets of the pearly cream landing on her inner thigh.

Struggling to breathe, Dante closed his eyes, robbed of the joy of ecstasy. Releasing her legs, he bent and scooped up his pants as he stepped away. Toya's legs wobbled when her feet touched the floor. Her hands splayed out behind her on the wall. Her caramel gaze was locked on his face. The puffiness of her lips he knew was caused by the vehemence of his kiss.

Stepping back, he put more distance between them. Guilt sliced at his conscience, watching the confusion in her bright eyes. Orgasm still pulsating from his flesh, he knew he had to close off those emotions.

He loved his wife with all of his heart. His soul. And hated her for breaking his heart.

Reaching into his inside jacket pocket, he grabbed the papers and tossed them on the table, the current of air extinguishing the candles. "They're all signed," he said, not attempting to disguise the contempt in his tone.

Latoya shook her head, still trying to catch her breath. She looked at her husband, his shoulders sagging. Agitated breaths scurried from his chest. He stared back at her, his midnight eyes cold.

Slowly, she tore her gaze from Dante's face and glanced at the stack of white folded papers. She didn't understand…

Oh, God… She closed her eyes. Swallowed against the tightness clogging her throat.

The divorce papers.

Air became stagnant in her lungs. For a moment her heart stopped, then accelerated. Tears dripped from her lower lashes. Rolled a silvery path down her cheeks.

He'd signed them. He hadn't even tried to talk to her. Clearly, he wanted out. Mustering her defenses, she opened her eyes.

Standing before her, his slacks gaped open revealing semi-hard cock, still slick with her juices. Fists clenched at his sides. Defeat and resignation etched his handsome features.

"They're signed," he repeated, his voice softer now.

How had he known? How had he gotten them? Licking her lips, Latoya tried to ease the dryness of her mouth. "You were going through my shit?"

He scoffed, shaking his head. "You had a flat this morning. I fixed it."

And gotten the spare from the trunk. Where she'd stashed away the divorce papers just in case she couldn't tempt her husband for a second time. She'd had them drawn up merely as a security blanket, but hoped she'd never actually have to use them.

Her knees shook. Leaning back against the wall for support, she whispered, "It's not—"

He cut her off. "Who is he?"

"What?"

"Who. Is. He?"

She shook her head. "You think I'm having an affair?"

"Isn't that what all this shit is about?"

She opened her mouth to speak, but he put his hand up. "Know what? Don't answer. I don't give a fuck." Slanting his head toward the papers resting on the table, he arched a brow. "You got what you wanted. I signed them." Turning, he walked away.

"Dante."

Long stride faltered, but didn't stall.

"Dante, where are you going?"

He glanced back. An angry smirk curled his luscious lips. "To wash this bitch off my dick."

A few moments later, she heard the bathroom door close firmly.

Her knees gave way and she crumbled to the floor. Drawing her legs up before her, she wrapped her arms around them, curling into the fetal position, quiet sobs shaking her entire body.

Her marriage was over and it was all her fault.

What had she done?

Chapter Three
A Groove that Lasts

ഐ

He'd turned into a fucking stalker. For the third straight day, he slowly drove down their street, just wanting to see if his wife was at home. The garage was closed. All the windows dark. The memory of her huddled on the floor, her slender body trembling haunted his dreams, robbing him of sleep. Making the days painful, the nights excruciatingly long.

Good. Let her experience some of the anguish he was feeling. She was the one who'd stepped out on him. Yet every time he reminded himself of the reason for the separation, he couldn't believe it. Not his girl. Not his sweet Latoya.

She wasn't there. He kept going, heading back to the hotel where he'd been staying since he'd left home.

* * * * *

Latoya shifted onto her side, propping a pillow under her cheek on the couch, then tucked her feet beneath the soft angora throw. Though both physically and emotionally exhausted, she'd been unable to sleep. Unable to eat. Had called in sick for the last few days from work. Not only would it have been impossible to have concentrated on her job, she was afraid to leave the house in case Dante came home while she was gone.

The tears all cried out, her eyes burned. Lack of sleep darkened the puffiness beneath. Her lids drooped, but visions of her husband standing rigid and angry before her caused her to open them again. The house was dim, illuminated only by the milky light of the moon that seeped through the open curtains. But she could make out the broken picture frame on the floor where she'd left it.

It wasn't the anger in his dark gaze that had crushed her. It was the pain. He'd accused her of unfaithfulness, but hadn't allowed her to deny it. She'd been a fool. A fool not to have gone after him. Demand that he listen. Tell him there was no man but him.

Only him.

She brushed her fingertips across the karat of ice held by platinum to her ring finger of her left hand. The metal felt cool and yet somehow reassuring.

Taking an unsteady breath, she searched her mind for ways to right her wrongs. To fix the damage lack of communication had caused. She wanted nothing more than to touch velvet skin. To hold him. To have him home where he belonged.

Gulping, Latoya felt ashamed. She'd turned their relationship into a game of tricks of seduction and secret secondary plans. Disgusted, she could hardly believe that she'd even seen an attorney and had those damned papers drawn up. Hell, what had she been thinking? How could she have resorted to such an extreme without sitting her man down and talking to him?

Now she had to fix things. Before the wounds of resentment were so deep they couldn't be healed. Lifting a notepad and pen, she scribbled her name over and over as she'd done when they'd first met.

Latoya Ross. Latoya Ross. Latoya Ross. Latoya Ross.

Ross. A name she'd gotten in matrimony. And intended to keep.

Sitting up and tossing the pad aside, she reached for the phone, pressing redial. Like all the other times over the last few days, his cell phone rang into voicemail and rather than leave a message she severed the connection. Knowing, too, that each call left an ID imprint on the receiving phone.

He'd know she called.

Leaning back onto the sofa, she lolled her head to the side and caught the lingering masculine scent of her husband's body.

A strangled sob tore from her lips and she turned her face more fully into the cushion. She was so damned tired. And yearning so badly for the tender embrace of her husband's arms.

Rolling her head to relieve the tension in her neck, her gaze halted in the dining room. On the folded papers resting on the table where Dante had thrown them.

"Those papers shouldn't exist." Dragging a full breath into her lungs, Latoya rose to her feet, then crossed the room, barefoot and wearing nothing but one of her husband's large undershirts. She reached for them, then hesitated. Fear tightened in her belly. Swiping a solitary tear, she focused on determination. Grabbing the divorce papers, she crumpled them in her hand then walked to the kitchen looking for a match.

Matches in hand, she retraced her steps back to the living room, then knelt on the floor in front of the fireplace. Feeling a weight ease from her chest, she didn't falter as she struck a flame, touched the corner, and watched the mother-fucker burn.

Dropping her chin to her chest, warmth spread across her cheeks. Lack of sleep made her body feel heavy, but she kept her gaze on the papers as they turned to ash.

Resolve potent.

She'd get her man back. Burning the papers was only the first step.

A tingle scurried down her spine. The wispy baby hairs on the nape of her neck lifted. There was a movement by the door.

Then she could hear him breathing. Her own halted. Slowly, Latoya lifted her chin and turned to look at him.

Dante stood by the door, his feet shoulder width apart, his hands hanging loosely at his sides. Keys gripped in one fist, cell phone in the other.

"Dante," she mouthed, unable to push out sound.

Dark eyes shifted to the fire. "What are you doing?"

"Burning them." Her voice broke saying those words.

Her husband stood motionless, his gaze fixed on the hearth

where fire ate away the pages, curling them, then turning them to ash. He still stared, even after all the fuel had been consumed and the flames sputtered and died. A raspy groan was emitted from his throat as he slowly turned his attention back to her.

Folding her hands in her lap, she wrung her fingers together so tightly her skin burned. "You're here."

"You called me."

She nodded.

"Why?"

"To talk," she whispered, her throat so thick with emotion forming words hurt.

Striding across the room, he closed the distance, then scooped her from the floor into his arms. He held there for a moment, pressed to his chest, his pulse throbbing beneath her cheek. Dark eyes settled on hers, intent and imploring. Saying nothing, he moved them to the couch and sat down, keeping her in his lap.

Brushing his delicious lips against her temple, he spoke softly. "So talk, baby."

Pride mattered not at all. Only her husband did. Only being in his arms. In his life. In his bed. Welcomed into his heart.

"I was wrong, Daddy."

He was silent, but he nuzzled the slope of her throat. Ran his tongue across her wildly rapid pulse. Kissed the sensitive skin below her ear.

"I was wrong," she whispered, turning in his lap to cup his face in her palms. "We needed to talk. Badly. Too much time would pass and we said nothing of value to each other. I needed you."

"I was here." His turned slightly and kissed her palm, then nipped playfully with his teeth.

"No, you were slipping away from me."

"I'm here, baby." He put a hand on the back of her head and with minimal pressure pulled her to him. She went willingly, accepting the tenderness of his kiss. He nibbled her bottom lip. Sucked it into his mouth. Gently nipped. "I'm here, Toya. Talk to me."

"I'm not having an affair."

He exhaled. Nodded. "I know."

"I don't want a divorce. I shouldn't have gotten the papers."

"Why did you, then?"

Latoya shifted to face him, straddling his muscular thighs. He touched her shoulder, tenderly ran his palm down her arm. Took her hand and entwined their fingers. His other hand lifted. With his fingertips, he outlined her lips.

Blinking back fresh tears, she calmed herself with his presence. "Days would go by when we hardly spoke a word to each other. Tired from long days, we'd lounge on the couch watching TV rather than asking how the other was doing. Kisses goodbye stopped. Kisses hello became infrequent." She paused. Her voice cracked as she went on. "We no longer made love."

"Why didn't you just tell me what was bothering you?"

Her eyes stung trying to hold back the tears. Her nose burned. She bit her bottom lip to stop it from trembling. "I was afraid."

"Afraid of what, baby?" he asked softly, gently caressing her jaw with his large hand.

"Afraid you didn't want me anymore."

Dante chuckled. Lifting his hips, he rolled them against the apex of his wife's spread legs so she could feel his hard-on. "I want you now."

Touching her lips, he felt her intake of breath. With fingers splayed down the feminine slope of her neck, he felt how her pulse shifted. Alluring caramel eyes melted his heart. The rhythm fast and hard.

He watched as she worked to swallow, her tone so uncertain when she whispered to him. "How do you want me?

Only in your bed?"

"No, Latoya Ross, I want you as my wife."

Her lids closed. Nostrils flared slightly.

One fat droplet of moisture rolled from each eye and snaked a silver trail down her cheeks to his hand. He dragged her forward, affectionately covering her lush lips that last time he'd been so carelessly brutal with. The kiss was tender. Poignant. Ending the kiss, he leaned his forehead on hers.

"I didn't think you loved me anymore."

"How could you think that?"

"You didn't tell me."

He sat her up, dropping his hands to her waist and ground his hips into hers, pressing the full length of his hardened dick against the damp heat of her pussy. "Baby, I've been better than telling you. I been showing you. I work hard for us, getting us this house so one day our children will grow up away from the ghettos. So that we can have a better life. So I can give you everything you've ever wanted. And, Toya, I come home to *you.*"

She nodded, but remained silent.

"I love you, girl, by making love."

Again, she said nothing as her hand slid down his chest, his abdomen trembling beneath his T-shirt. Her fingers toyed with the hem, brushed low against his gut. His cock throbbed in response, hard enough he was pretty damn sure she could feel it. She scooted forward just slightly rubbing her clit along him.

Tightening his jaw, raw desire consumed him. "I'm sorry if I hurt you the other night."

"You were upset and only hurt me by leaving."

"I'm sorry, baby."

A smile brightened her eyes and that damned sexy tongue of hers brushed along her upper teeth. Fingers crept beneath his shirt, inciting his lust as she swirled her delicate fingers in the line of hair that plunged from his gut to the base of his dick. His balls drew close to his body as his heart rate leapt.

"Daddy, can you show me now?"

"Huh?"

She smiled a wickedly seductive grin. "Show me how you love me."

Dante laughed. Closing the distance, he slanted his mouth over hers and pressed his tongue between her teeth. Greeted by the saltiness of her tears, his heart ached. But she was sweet inside, so warm and alluring.

She blossomed, kissing him back so thoroughly he thought he might explode. Then she changed the pace on him, from languid to frenzied. Her breathing sharpened into pants. Her hands delved into his sweatpants, beneath his boxers and closed around his shaft, testing every ounce of his restraint.

Trying to slow her down before he came in her hands, he held her forearms as she curled demanding fingers around him and stroked. But she shrugged off his contact and whimpered onto his tongue. Shoving at his pants, she moved them down just far enough to free him, her thumb finding the bead of pre-cum on his plum-shaped head.

His wife lifted onto her knees, bringing him to the folds of her heat. A growl grumbled from his lips as she teased his body by rotating her hips along his rigid length, pressing against her clit. Slick arousal intoxicated him, she was so damned wet.

She rose higher, then took him in, giving him only an inch. His body trembled, her insistent hands fondling his sac, the throbbing vein running up his cock, caressing his head with the tightness of her pussy.

Grabbing her hips, he fought the need to shove her fully onto him, to get all the way inside. But he relented to the game his wife played. This was about Toya. About showing her how much he loved her. Tonight, he'd fuck her just the way she wanted.

In a siren's dance, she rotated her hips in a circle, moaning even as she kissed him. Her inner thighs trembled against his.

Yet she held her position, tormenting him and enjoying it.

Then, sucking his tongue into her mouth, she spread her knees and accepted him fully, thrusting downward onto every thick inch of him. Crying out his name. Welcoming him into her sopping heat.

Oh, hell, yeah!

He was home.

About the Author

෨

Multi-published author Renee Luke believes in keeping-it-real erotic romances that feature funky urban characters who get their groove on and give up their hearts. She strives to write stories that both stimulate physically and satisfy emotionally. She believes in happily-ever-afters and found her own in California with her fine-ass man and their four damn-cute children.

Renee welcomes comments from readers. You can find her website and email address on her author bio page at www.ellorascave.com.

WEREWOLF IN L.A.

Marianne LaCroix

Chapter One
Hollywood, California, 1941

෩

"Action!" called Melville Smith, B-movie director extraordinaire. Of course, no one at International Star Studios would ever tell Mr. Smith he created B movies. Most of the cast saw his entire film production process as a joke, but Smith took his job very seriously. The low- to no-budget films were the bread and butter of ISS, but he refused to accept any downgrade to his creative genius — at least it was genius in his eyes.

Estelle Lane awaited her cue on stage left as the scene from *Blood Hound* played out before her. She was a queen of the B-movie lot, and she liked it. She might not be in the same class as the Hollywood prima donnas like Vivien Leigh, Katherine Hepburn or Lauren Bacall, but Estelle had a talent those ladies couldn't match. And as an actress in her late twenties, Estelle was in her pinnacle years in Hollywood. She was ripe in beauty and agility to compete for parts. In the B movies, the parts would continue as she aged, but the scene time would be less — as would the pay.

She watched as her leading man, or chump in her opinion, played out the scene. How was she supposed to convince an audience she was in love with such an asshole? *Acting.* Her talent came into play every time she was matched with Donald Valentino. The idiot thought he was the next Errol Flynn. If only. The man was handsome and perfectly built, but had no acting talent. He had the personality of a flea. His dreams would only be realized on the casting couch.

Donald's slicked-back hair brushed the back of his collar, and his pencil-thin mustache was a tad too thin. He had hazel eyes and a perfectly capped smile. Sporting an athletic frame and snug-fitting trousers, he was the model of the Hollywood hopeful actor. Just like the hundreds of other men in L.A.

"I have a houseful of dinner guests and you are telling me I can't let anyone leave tonight because of a legend?" Donald's line was her cue.

"What do you mean we can't go home?" She walked into the scene in her black velvet evening gown that dipped in the back, and the elegantly coiffed hair. She was playing the love interest, the innocent yet sophisticated debutante who captured the eye of a rich British lord.

"Ah, Miss Ashton, please, come and join us," Donald's character, Lord Williamson, said to her. When he laid his hand upon her, her skin crawled. She fought her personal reactions and smiled.

"What is this about a legend?" she asked as she took a seat on the couch in the mock study.

"It isn't so much a legend, Miss Ashton. The wolf is very real." Peter Bennett, an older actor playing Lord Devon, said his line in a grave voice. Very dramatic.

"This is insane. Wolves don't walk around the Scottish moors at night looking for victims," Donald replied.

"What wolf?" she asked, opening the film for the revelation of the back story, most of which would be edited in later from footage shot elsewhere.

"Cut! Print!" Melville rose from his canvas folding chair throne and called out over his players. "Okay, take a ten-minute break while we set up for the next scene."

As she began to walk off to her dressing room, Donald called out. "Estelle, can I talk to you for a moment?"

She groaned inwardly. "Donald, our breaks are few. I want to go and relax for ten minutes. The next scene is one of mine."

He followed along behind her regardless. He really was persistent. "Estelle, the tabloids have us as dating. The studio developed a big push for us as a couple. I think we should go on out on the town tonight and feed the gossip columns. Think of the free publicity for both of us."

She snickered. "You mean publicity for *you*. I don't want to go out with you, Donald. I've told you that before. If I go out to be seen with you, that is on company time. That's part of the job."

He grabbed her arm tightly and she recognized anger in his eyes. "You will do as I tell you if you want to get anywhere in this town."

"I believe the lady said no, Don," a deep voice said.

Her eyes met the darkness of the stranger's, who stood only two feet away. He stepped from the shadows and her breath caught.

He was tall, muscular—and covered in hair. He was made up as the werewolf for the movie. Obviously hours were taken in applying the mask to his face. Yet it couldn't hide the striking man beneath the rubber and hair. He had an air, an aura about him that exuded power, strength, and control.

"What, a stuntman thinks he can interrupt something not concerning him? Move along, wolf-man." Donald said to the man Estelle couldn't tear her eyes from.

The man moved in close to Donald, his height towering over the actor by a few inches. He was an intimidating figure of a man. "I think you may regret ticking me off. You better move on to your dressing room before I make your makeup artist have to hide something very unsightly."

Don considered a moment, and then visibly backed down. He took a step backwards and breathed, "You're probably ugly as hell, which is why you have to hide behind a mask and makeup. Just remember who the star really is in this movie, wolf-man." With that, Don turned and stalked to his dressing room.

"Thank you for that," she said once she found her voice. Her body was humming in reaction. "He repulses me, and the studio making up a relationship for the gossip papers is difficult for me to keep up. I refuse to go out with him on my own time."

"You should tell them you don't want to do the ruse anymore. It is kind of, well, it is easy to see you aren't happy on his arm at premieres."

"I'm Estelle, what's your name?" She offered her hand and gasped at the contact of flesh upon flesh. His heat caressed her skin in a welcome embrace.

"Jack Butler. I'm the new stuntman here at International Star Studios."

"That would explain why I've never seen you before." He continued to hold her hand and she enjoyed his comforting hold.

"I don't usually talk with the actors off stage."

"And why is that?" She took a hesitant step forward just to get a little closer.

What did he look like under the mask? He radiated appeal, raw animalistic sexual appeal. And it zeroed in on her pussy, now aching to be petted by this stranger.

"Because…because not many people understand me."

She moved closer still, her body now touching along his. The contact was electric, and she slowly breathed in his spicy scent. The throb increased at her clit. "And how do you feel about talking with me now?" Her voice was breathy, heavy with her growing desire. Since when was she ever turned on by a man she just met?

"I think you're playing a dangerous game here, Miss Lane. You don't know me."

She tilted up her face to his. "I think I want to find out."

Electricity crackled about them, she clearly felt it in the air between them. He leaned forward, his lips mere inches from hers. "Want to crawl into the bed of a wolf, Miss Lane?"

She grasped his shirt as she moved to him, her body a heated puzzle piece finding the perfect fit. "Yes," she breathed.

When his lips touched hers, hesitant at first, she felt the jolt of contact course through her veins with each beat of her racing heart. With her sharp intake of breath, his kiss turned demanding. Mouths ground together in a newfound passion. He urged her lips apart and at her moan, his tongue dove into the sweetness of her mouth. He held her securely at the shoulders as he plundered her mouth, primal desire fueling the flames building between them.

She wanted him closer, much closer. Wrapping her one leg about his, she heard him moan as he moved his hand to her thigh and pulled her to him.

Her cunt was hot and weeping with want, her clit pulsated with need. She rubbed her lust-driven body against his hard, powerful frame as their tongues danced in tempo with her increased heartbeat.

He held on to her thigh, raising it higher, and she ground her pelvis against his. The skirt of her dress bunched at her waist, her crotch rubbed wonderfully against his straining cock within his pants.

He groaned as she panted, thrusting her hips against the bulge, the fabric-covered rod pressed against her swollen clit and she whimpered against his kisses.

He pulled his mouth from hers and he gasped, "Estelle." He nibbled her neck, her sensitive skin tingling beneath his lips. "Ever been fucked all night long, little Miss B-movie queen?"

Then a gasp from behind her snapped her from her blinding ecstasy of the moment. She was making out with a stuntman dressed like a werewolf, albeit a bad rendition of one, but this was a low-budget film.

"Hussy."

She recognized Donald's voice immediately.

She lowered her leg and straightened her dress. All the while Jack held her to his side in a protective embrace. Was it protective, or was it possessive? Either way, she appreciated the secure warmth of his body pressed to her.

"So, I'm not good enough to go to dinner with, but he is good enough for a quickie fuck while on a break? Two-bit whore."

Without a word, Jack moved in a flash and threw a punch to Don's jaw. The unexpected force dropped the actor on his ass, grasping his jaw in pain.

"Don't you *ever* speak to Miss Lane in such a manner. I ever hear you call her that again, I will make sure you don't work for a week…or more."

By then a small crowd of the crew and a few of the bit players had gathered to watch Don sent sprawling on the floor by a very angry stuntman.

"Melville! I demand this man be fired immediately!" Don sounded panicked. As strong as he was, he'd never be a match for Jack's strength.

The aging director arrived on the scene and quickly took in the situation.

Before he could say anything, Don demanded, "I want this man fired!" He pointed to Jack who had moved back to Estelle's side and kept an arm about her waist.

"I don't have time for macho nonsense on the set. Donald…you're relieved for the day. Go home." He turned to Estelle and said, "Go to makeup and fix your face and hair. Your scene is next." And then to Jack he just sniffed and said, "Try not to break his face."

Fifteen minutes later Estelle stood refreshed and ready on set. She couldn't help but be bothered by the encounter with the stuntman. What got into her to act like…like a hussy? Was Don right in calling her that? She'd never thrown herself at a stranger before, but there was an inner voice within her soul urging her onward. She needed some sort of connection to the sensual appeal of him. *Jack.*

Jack was in this scene and as Melville went over again what he was looking for in the shot, she stole a glance at him. His mask stayed perfectly in place. Must be glued on tight. But then it did take two hours for such a transformation to look passable. His wolfish look was where most of the money for this flick went.

Then a thought struck her. Could it be that Jack was paid better than Don? She didn't make a mint on this job, but someone could. If Don found out the stuntman made more than the star that would make for difficulties fueled by jealousy. There had to be more to Don's anger than just a stuntman kissing her. And what a kiss it was!

Jack's eyes met hers and a bolt of recognition shot through her body. What was it about him that made her heart leap and her clit throb?

"All right folks, this is the scene where Miss Ashton sees the wolf-man out the window. Miss Lane, you step up to the window like you are listening to the legend being told. We'll be adding in footage separately. Let's try to get this in one shot. Time and money are at a minimum. Okay, now, action."

They played out their scene and when she saw Jack in the window, Estelle displayed her special talent—her Fay Wray scream. Of course no scream would be complete without the overacted horror body language—hands thrown to the sides of her face, panicky and exaggerated. It was a must for the B movies.

"Cut! Print! Okay folks, that's a wrap for the day. Tomorrow we'll shoot the kidnapping scene," Melville announced before turning to his production assistant to discuss his plans for the next filming day.

"Want to go out for dinner tonight, Estelle?" Jack asked from behind the window stage prop. He'd opened the window and leaned on the sill.

Once again her breath caught. Sinfully sexy in his body language, she was drawn in by his raw bestial aura. "Will I get to see you without the mask?"

He smiled. "Anything the lady wishes." Then he added, "It's going to take them some time to get this off of me in one piece, so how about we meet at the stage six entrance in about an hour?"

"Sure."

"Think you'd know me without the facial hair and claws?" he chuckled.

"I'm sure I will know you anywhere." Her legs weakened, knowing she'd recognize him just by her body's response.

Chapter Two

ഔ

Jack was outside stage six when Melville came out to go home for the evening.

"Jack, hope your first day was good," the director said.

"Thanks, Mel. It was better than I hoped for."

The older man scratched his balding head as he studied Jack. "Waiting for Miss Lane?"

"She agreed to go to dinner with me tonight."

Melville nodded knowingly. "Be sure to be a gentleman. I stuck out my neck to get you on this film."

"And I appreciate the chance to work with her. To think, after two years of watching her from afar, I finally got to talk to her." Jack had hoped Estelle would find him attractive. He'd been dreaming of her for so long, she'd become a fantasy woman. When she held her body against him, he nearly came unglued. "That Don...he ticks me off. I can't believe he called her those things."

"I told you Don was an ass. He's a pretty face that sells tickets to female fans. He was forced on me by the studio heads. If I had my way, Basil Rathbone would be in this picture." Melville straightened his sport coat and added, "Miss Lane is a beautiful woman, and I don't approve of the studio making her play out an affair for the gossipmongers. It's time for her to be with a man worthy of her. Studio promotion be damned. Hell, the picture will do better if it got out the starlet was dating the mysterious wolf-man."

"I appreciate your help. I really didn't think she'd pay me any attention."

Melville smiled and said, "I knew you two would hit it off."

"We'll see."

"I saw how disheveled she was during the break. I don't think you have anything to worry about." With a smile Melville wished him a good night.

Alone, Jack began to wonder if she reconsidered.

"Hope you haven't waited long. I had to visit wardrobe to return the gown I wore today. It has to be cleaned for tomorrow's shoot." She appeared at the entrance and he was taken aback at her simple beauty. Without the thick stage makeup, Estelle had applied a simpler look. Her hair was still swept up in the style she had for the filming, but it was classic and modern. Her lips were by far her best feature, and she wore a dark red lipstick, accentuating their full beauty. Kissable. And he wanted those lips just for him.

"No, not long."

"Where are we going?" Her smile warmed him, and her voice calmed the beast within.

"The Brown Derby. Ever been there?"

"Oh yes. I take my mother there when she comes out to visit. She is such a movie fan. She loves sitting back to see who walks in next."

He laughed and gently touched her elbow to guide her out the studio lot. "Ever see anyone famous?"

"We saw Clark Gable one night. That was a thrill, I have to tell you." She giggled at the memory. "My mom turned into a lovesick teenager. She did get his autograph, and she treasures it."

"I bet. My personal thrill was when I saw Boris Karloff one time. I was so awed I could hardly put two words together." He smiled and asked, "Who would be your thrilling moment if you saw them?"

She walked beside him, her hand gently curled at the crook of his arm. Her welcoming gesture made him yearn to hold her. She deserved to be treated like royalty, to be spoiled, cherished…loved.

She was silent as they walked, then she finally said, "I'm really not sure. Isn't that strange?"

"Not at all." Outside the studio gates, Jack indicated to the limo awaiting curbside. "Only the best for my lady." He hoped she'd be impressed and he wasn't disappointed. He was rewarded with a quick kiss on the cheek.

Within the limo, she pressed close to his side. "Thank you for this. I've never ridden in a limousine before."

He wrapped his hand about hers and relished the warm comfort of her touch. "I wanted to be sure to make tonight special."

Laying her head on his shoulder, she sighed. "I have a feeling this will be a night to remember."

"I figure after dinner we can visit Grauman's Chinese Theater and walk in the concrete footsteps of the stars."

Her hold on his arm tightened and his cock jumped. Damn, if he got any harder, he wouldn't be able to hold back the urges to take her—here and now. Sniffing the air, he smelled her excitement, her honeyed cream moistening her panties. Oh dear God, how could he fight for control when her feminine perfume called to him?

"I think that would be wonderful. A true romantic Hollywood date." She tilted her face to him.

He could almost taste her lips, sweet and wet. He moaned as he shifted his seat. "Estelle," he whispered, his mouth a breath away from hers. "You continue to move closer to me like you are, and we may not make our reservations tonight at the Derby."

A shot of desire coursed through her veins. "There's always the ride there."

* * * * *

Estelle was in awe. Jack was, by far, the most appealing man she'd ever seen. He had a rugged, masculine face, not the typical soft, romantic profile of Hollywood actors. His slight shadow of a beard across his chin added to his strong appearance. His muscular build intensified his irresistible attractiveness. Dressed in a smart-looking charcoal gray suit and tie, he was completely opposite from when she'd seen him previously. He was drop-dead gorgeous.

Not only was Jack incredibly handsome, even better than she anticipated, he had a romantic heart. No man she ever dated here in Hollywood even suggested such a romantic evening. Dinner at the Brown Derby, and then a walk at Grauman's Chinese theater? Falling in love with him would be so easy.

Wait, she said love? Over a meal and a stroll? It was more than any other man ever wanted from her, usually it was a quick burger at a drive-in joint and fondling in the backseat of their car. Nights like that usually left Estelle feeling empty. Sex was good on occasion, but nothing engulfing, no electric passion to keep her fires burning past the goodnight kiss. Hell, she hardly ever went out with such men again. Could it be that Jack was second date material? And third? And fourth? And more…much more.

He literally wrapped around her as she sat next to him. She inched to him, sure to have him close. Her body yearned for contact. His body called to hers in a silent bidding, and his voice excited her already on-edge libido.

Need was talking. Need for him to fill her. She wanted to become one with him, a joining of bodies and souls.

He closed the spare few inches between their mouths and kissed her. Hot passion inflamed her. Her hands clasped at him, drawing him near. There was nothing gentle in the kiss, a primal want feeding the fire burning, threatening to spread out of control.

She didn't want control. She wanted wild.

Lacing her fingers through his black hair, she moaned into his kiss. When he reached down her leg and raised the hem of her dress, she allowed him to go further.

"I don't want to hurt you," he whispered, breaking his deep kisses to seduce her with his lips tantalizing hers.

"You won't hurt me. Please, touch me."

"I've wanted you for so long. Seeing you on the screen—I had to meet you."

She reached down and guided his hand beneath her dress. His palm, roughened from true work, felt heavenly against her sensitive skin along the inside of her thighs. "Don't talk, just touch me."

At the first brush of his thumb over her cotton-covered clit, she cried out against his mouth.

"Are we going too fast?" he growled, seemingly unsure of his actions, even though his thumb gently drew small circles over her crotch.

Her answer was a possessive kiss. She tasted him, her tongue delving into his mouth, relentless, lustful. He held her tighter to him, answering her passion and increased the pressure of his touch along her nubbin. It was torture, the thin fabric separating his fingers from her swelling flesh. Delightful, yet painful ecstasy.

Her fingers were curled through his dark hair, pulling him closer still. His free hand molded her body with expertise. Lips danced together, tongues tasting, testing, exploring. She was on fire, set to explode at any moment.

Then he grasped her breast with one hand while the other continued its sweet caress over her clit. He squeezed and she whimpered in surrender. Just when his thumb and forefinger pinched her hardened nipple into a point, she shattered. The inferno blazed brightly as her body climaxed within his arms.

She cried out against his kisses, and he continued stroking her, heightening her pleasure. She rode out the contractions that seemed to begin at the center of her being and radiate out to all her extremities. She felt the orgasm within every cell of her body.

The stars before her eyes began to die down as her muscles relaxed. He held her close to him, and she was aware of his ragged breathing. "Are you all right?" she asked, touching the side of his face with her fingertips.

He turned his face away and breathed deeply. Oh God, did she disgust him with coming so easily?

"I'm sorry," she said as she began to pull away.

But he held her firm to him, his scent of musk filling her senses. "No reason to be sorry," he said in a controlled voice before turning his face back to her. "It was hard not to just fuck you right here and now."

"Really? You aren't upset with how — how I acted?"

"Upset? Not on your life. I just wish…" An inner torment reflected within his stormy gray eyes. What was it about this man that made him so unusual, so unlike any other man she'd ever known?

"Wish what? Is there something wrong, Jack?"

"I'm not like other men."

"I know that already."

He sighed. "I put you in danger if I make love to you."

"Danger? What sort of danger?" This was beginning to alarm her, even as her body still hummed from her recent climax.

He brushed back her hair from her face and tucked her head beneath his chin so she nuzzled his throat. "Let's not think on it now. I want to enjoy having you by my side."

They rode the rest of the way to the restaurant in silence, but Estelle's mind raced with questions. What could be the danger he spoke of?

Chapter Three

So absorbed in his obsession with Estelle, he'd forgotten how intense emotion unleashed the beast within his soul. Sexual excitement usually awakened the wolfen part, but never like this. Holding her, bringing her to ecstasy not only awakened his animalistic soul, but it clawed fiercely for dominance. If it were a full moon tonight, Jack doubted he'd be able to fight back. The alpha wanted complete control, and could possibly put Estelle in danger.

Jack was bitten ten years ago while on a camping trip with two college buddies. They all wanted to spend a holiday trekking through the wilderness of the Rocky Mountains. They fished, relaxed and drank beer. It was a glorious time for men who enjoyed the outdoors. But then one night things went terribly wrong.

While they sat around the campfire, drinking way too much beer, they heard the howl of a wolf in the distance. While the sound wasn't entirely unusual, the appearance of one in their camp was definitely unusual. Jack never forgot the look of evil in the animal's red eyes—supernatural and dangerous. The wolf growled at the men staggering to stand. The wolf was quickly backed by two more wolves.

"Rabies, you think?" Jeff, one of his buddies, asked with a slur.

"Has to be," Jon, a football quarterback star, said in a shaky voice. It was unnerving to hear the big man's voice quiver in building fear.

The next moments were a blur to Jack. He only remembered waking up in the morning outside the camp, bitten on his shoulder. Back at the camp, Jack found his friends both badly injured from the freak attack. Jack, having the less severe wounds, hiked back to the car and sought help at a nearby forest ranger station. When he returned to the campsite with help, Jeff and Jon were gone. He'd never heard or seen Jon and Jeff ever again. The authorities declared the men as "assumed dead" but Jack knew they were still out there. He never found out who the werewolves were, but he was sure someday he'd cross paths with them.

A week later, Jack discovered the power of the full moon and began to transform.

He'd become a werewolf, controlled by a beast clawing for dominance. With the coming of a full moon, the beast gained more power. Only through self-control did Jack learn to fight back his animalistic soul. In time he discovered the strength of his own emotional reactions and the connection to the beast.

As he held Estelle while she climaxed, his wolfen side waged battle for supremacy. It wanted freedom—power to fuck the woman it recognized as its mate. Her scent of sexual excitement and satisfaction called to the beast within. He almost lost the battle as she cried out, her body shuddering in his arms.

Once they arrived at the Brown Derby, Jack regained control over himself. Her soft body so readily molded to his in the car was a temptation. He wanted her, not just because the wolf demanded it, his heart whispered to him. Love and complete devotion was the price he needed from her. Would a woman so adored by men find it in her heart to love a man who was ruled by a beast?

At the restaurant the maitre d' greeted them and sat them in a quiet corner. From their table, they could easily watch the stars walk in.

Jack was always awed by the sheer glamour of the Brown Derby. The exterior was the shape of a gigantic derby hat. Inside, the walls were lined with signed caricatures of stars from silent era greats like Rudolph Valentino to the modern-day stars on the rise like Ingrid Bergman. The tables were lit by soft candlelight, and polished woods along with fine burgundy velvet curtains added a classic richness to the simple décor. The restaurant's centerpiece was the ornate oval bar. These all combined to make the Derby the place to meet the talent of Hollywood.

Estelle remained quiet, seemingly absorbed in her menu.

"Estelle?" he asked.

She looked up to his face locking her gaze with his. "Yes?"

"I'm sorry if I made you feel uncomfortable. That wasn't my intention."

She simply nodded.

He reached across the table and touched her hand. The jolt at the contact made him inhale sharply. "I really like you, Estelle. Much more than any other woman I've ever known. I am just afraid of losing you by doing something stupid."

"I like you too, Jack. I want you to know that you can trust me. This is not a fling for me. I don't do one-night affairs. I wouldn't be here tonight if I didn't think you were special. I want to get to know you."

They went on to have a quiet dinner together. He was relieved how they managed to ease back into being comfortable together over a simple act like eating. At least his emotions were not purely sexual. He loved hearing she liked him and wanted to learn more about him. He just hoped when his secret was revealed, it wouldn't rip her to pieces.

"So, how did you come to be in Hollywood doing low-budget horror movies?" he asked taking a bite of his rare steak. It practically melted in his mouth, appeasing the beast's hungry yearning.

"I fell in love with the movies when I was small. I remember going to the movies every Saturday afternoon to watch Lon Chaney in *Phantom of the Opera* and in *Hunchback of Notre Dame*. When sound hit, I raced to watch Bela Lugosi as Dracula and Boris Karloff as a walking corpse in *The Mummy*. I loved the horror movies. If it had a good monster, I loved it. While my friends swooned over Rudolph Valentino or Clark

Gable, I was cheering on for the latest monster film to make it to the local theater."

"But what made you come to California to act in the movies?"

She chuckled, a sweet sound that made his cock tingle to life. "I was always interested in theater, and I was playing Mina in a college production of *Dracula* when a talent scout found me. Said I had passable acting skills, but my face would put me on the screen. So, I came to Hollywood with stars in my eyes and a suitcase of dreams. Took some acting lessons and had photo shoots. Got a few bit parts that eventually led upward on the studio ladder of success." Shrugging she added, "I never cared if I made it big, I just wanted to live comfortably. And doing it in movies I grew up watching, that makes it all worthwhile. I get to be opposite vampires and werewolves on a daily basis."

If she only knew…

* * * * *

Walking in the moonlight with Jack was probably the highlight of her night. Dinner was enjoyable, and Estelle felt like she found a truly wonderful man. The sexual excitement that had bubbled over in the limousine on the way to the Derby simply made the air crackle between them as the night progressed. She was unsure how to react to his indication of danger. There was none as far as she could tell. Perhaps he was being cautious of her heart? Her love life, not being stellar in any sense of the meaning, couldn't get any worse than having to pretend to the media she was involved with Don.

Melville was right. He'd visited her dressing room as she got ready for her date with Jack. "Estelle, I think you need to put an end to the charade of the relationship with Don. It isn't going to help the film any." She didn't think anything of his remark until he added before leaving, "Jack is a good man. He'd treat you right. And a relationship, a true one, would help the film when it is released."

A glance at Jack outside Grauman's, slipping his feet over the concrete footprints of her idol, Lon Chaney Sr., and she knew Jack was *the one*.

Her body was on fire despite the cool evening breeze, and nothing could extinguish the fire — except Jack.

"Estelle, you said you watched a lot of Lon Chaney, right?" He sounded like an excited child, bursting with a piece of news.

"Yeah, loved how he brought life to the Phantom. That's my favorite."

"Well, I hear his son, Lon Chaney Jr., is going to be the wolf-man in the Universal picture."

"Oh, so you have special privilege to know this?"

He laughed and the sound vibrated through her. "Yeah, well, being a wolf-man, I would get to hear this kind of news first. I think it is cool."

"Think it will hurt the opening for *Blood Hound*?"

"Doubt it. There's a market for both films. More than likely, *The Wolfman* will help the release of *Blood Hound*." He laughed as he reached for her. "Besides, *Blood Hound* has you as the leading lady. I know I'd pay for several tickets just to watch you over and over on the screen."

Her body pressed to his, she felt the heat pour off him, wrapping about her in an invisible embrace. "Jack, I—I need—"

His lips covered her without a sound. He kissed her gently, a soft playing of lips together in an ancient dance of love.

"Estelle, if I make love to you," he whispered against her lips. "I may become — something."

"What? Just tell me, Jack." She curled her fingers through his black hair, pulling him down to her mouth harder.

He answered her urging and deeply kissed her. Colors swirled behind her eyelids as she fell into the passion building between them. Heat surged and she felt the undeniable hard-on of his cock through his pants, rubbing against her belly. She wanted to feel his skin. The need to touch his flesh urged her onward as the kisses grew wilder.

Moments later, he broke the kiss and held her at arm's length. Breath labored, he said, "Can you take a beast in bed, Estelle?"

"Jack, I want you to be a beast. Ravish me, take me." Her body surged with life, writhing with unanswered desire. The brief release in the limo was just a teaser, she needed more. Skin to skin. Sweat dripping into more sweat.

Something flashed in his eyes. With a snarl, he lifted her into his arms. She whimpered as she wrapped her arms about his neck. He moved swiftly, not back to the car, but along the sidewalks, through the alleys.

"Jack, I need you. Say you'll love me tonight." She nibbled his ear and got an answering growl.

"I'll love you always. As of now, you are mine."

Heat pooled between her thighs and she moaned. He stopped and leaned over to sniff her crotch. "Oh fuck," he murmured. "You smell so sweet and ripe. I just want to eat you for dessert."

"Oh yes," she cried.

He started again, but took a turn down a side street dimly lit by a street lamp. It was the side entrance to a restaurant and no one was in sight.

"I have to taste you—*now*." He set her down and backed her against the brick exterior of the building. "No one will see us," he whispered.

"I don't even care if they do." She pulled him close, his body now pinning her against the wall. "Just fuck me with your tongue, Jack." Another woman had taken the place of Estelle the starlet. This was Estelle the sex-hungered woman.

He kissed her, bruising and possessive. His hands roughly held her, and she loved it. He continued on to lick her neck— working downward. She guided his head in her frenzy to feel him.

She needed to come. She wanted his mouth upon her clit, working the nubbin into a hard point. It ached for his touch, and now she was going to get it.

Oh yes, touch me, tease me, she thought. She liked his command of her body, and it reacted to his superior strength. Domination of her senses, her body — *oh yes*!

He went to his knees and pulled up her skirt. With a sharp tug, her panties ripped off, exposing her pussy to the night air. Lifting her thigh over his shoulder, she felt the air caress her center, but not for long. He dove in and covered her straining clit with his mouth.

She held on to his head as his tongue laved along the feminine opening. It gaped open for him and he answered the silent plea to fill the cavern inviting him. Like a man starved, he fed upon her juices. Her hips moved in rhythm, craving more of his beastlike feast.

Then he slowed, flicking his tongue lightly over her clit. She thought she'd die from the easier pace until he slipped a finger through her slit. Honeyed with her wetness, his fingers slid up into her cunt and she gasped, bunching her fists in his hair.

One finger was joined by another as he continued his oral assault upon her body. No one ever made her body abandon control like this. Sweet torture, just when she began to climb to a point of no return, he eased into soft nibbles of her clit and labia. He'd bring her down from the heights only to begin to build up the ecstasy once again.

When she thought she'd die of the pleasure, he pushed his thumb through the tight opening of her anus. She cried out as the orgasm hit her. Every muscle seemed to contract and convulse in tempo to his mouth's sucking her nubbin.

A screaming orgasm. She'd never experienced the feat until now. And now she could say she had done so in the side alley next to a restaurant and an apartment building in L.A.

Her whole body rocked and lights danced across her vision as she rode out her climax.

As she began to come down from the pinnacle of pleasure, she sighed with a smile, "Beast."

"My beauty," he replied gruffly against her belly, embracing her sated body.

"We aren't done, are we?" she asked while stroking his hair. She loved what he'd done to her, and didn't want it to end.

"That was only the previews, sweetheart."

Chapter Four

ꙮ

Seemed he really knew the alley as it was the one right next to his apartment. He carried her up the fire escape stairs and entered through the window.

"You always keep your window open to go through?" she asked when he placed her on his bed.

"Well, the ladies in the building like to gossip. They spot you, that gives them material for weeks." He caressed her check with his thumb. "You mean more to me than a one-night fling, or fodder for gossipmongers."

She smiled and he leaned down to kiss her gently.

Soft lips against hers, she thought she'd found heaven on earth with Jack. Not only was he sensitive and sexy, he was an animal during sex. Well, oral sex. But what would it be like having his cock fill her, stretching her walls to the limit as he pumped in and out?

She moaned at the vision.

He backed away and began to strip off his suit coat. The wild man revealed beneath the conservative exterior.

She glanced about the room and saw a very comfortable studio flat. One large room, it had everything a man could need to live. The kitchen was tucked on one side with a bar separating it from the rest of the room. Stools lined the bar, a single man's way to eat and run, she supposed. Farther into the room was a sitting room with an overstuffed chair and matching sofa. They hardly looked like they were ever used. And then there was the sleeping area where she lay. The bed was huge, king-size, with the sheets pulled back. He obviously didn't make his bed in the morning. The mattress against her back was firm yet comfortable.

Then she turned her eyes on him as he continued to undress beside a wooden rocking chair that sat between the bed and a chest of drawers. He carefully draped his coat on the back of the chair then slipped off his tie. The act of him undressing was strangely alluring and Estelle lay back to enjoy the simple daily activity turned sensual.

He began to unbutton his shirt and she moaned, drawing his attention. He grinned and popped the next button open. Hint of hair lay beneath the cotton oxford, and her fingers itched to run over his muscled chest.

"No undershirt, Jack?" she crooned as he removed his shirt.

"Does Gable wear undershirts?" he asked, referring to the movie *It Happened One Night*. In the movie Clark Gable removed his shirt to a bare chest. He practically destroyed the underwear industry overnight—men wanted to be like Gable and stopped wearing undershirts too.

She chuckled and began to move across the bed to pull off her dress. "I usually wear underpants, but I don't have any at the moment."

He unfastened his belt and unzipped his fly. "Can't imagine how that happened. Did you meet with some beast in an alley?" he asked with a smile.

"A beast of a man, a wolf-man," she giggled, tossing her dress to the chair. Clad in only her bra, she felt exposed—sexy for him as his eyes feasted upon her.

"I am your wolf, Estelle. And you're my mate." He pulled off his pants and kicked off his shoes.

He wore boxers, and she loved it. His body was toned just as she thought, all powerful sinew. His height, over six feet, made him an intimidating figure of strength. Yet she knew he would be nothing but tender to her.

Unclasping her bra, she admitted, "I don't do this type of thing with just anyone, Jack." She let her bra fall away from her breasts as she sat on her knees upon the bed.

He tilted up her face. "Neither do I." He kissed her, deeply, wholly.

Her breasts tightened and her nipples brushed against the hair upon his chest. Hardened points, they throbbed with need.

Her juices flowed and her clit strained for his touch. He pressed closer to her and she loved the feel of his naked flesh along hers. Plunging his fingers through her hair, he held her head steady as he continued his sensual assault, his tongue diving into her mouth, feeding the desires building between them. Hot steel rubbed along her belly and she groaned. Reaching down, she pulled off his underwear and grasped his surging cock.

Breaking their kiss, he howled in pleasure. Seeing the power over his reactions from her touch, she traced down his chest to his abdomen with her tongue. Salty sweat began to form on his body as he fought for control. She was determined to break that — right now.

He stood next to the bed and she crouched low, her mouth mere millimeters from his cock. The lovely bulbous head, purplish and engorged, topped a thick erection. It was a work of art. When a bead of cum pearled upon the very tip, her mouth watered.

"Oh God, Estelle," he panted as she flicked her tongue over the bead.

"Delicious," she cooed before licking it again.

His breath became jagged when she gently took the head into her mouth. Oh-so tenderly, she worshipped the velvety surface — hard yet welcoming.

He tried to urge her to hurry, but she refused. His grip on her head became a small battle of power as she tasted and teased his penis. Running her tongue over the length of steel then once again closing her lips over the head, she enjoyed the giving of pleasure to this incredible man.

He moved his hips, thrusting his cock into her mouth and she allowed the penetration. Taking in his length, she savored the sensation, and his spurring on her ministrations. She loved the power, the control over him. He'd taken control before in the alley of her body, but now was her time. This was her chance to express her heart. His cock beat in rhythm into her mouth and she sucked him deep inside.

"Baby, no—no—oh God, don't stop." He was pulling her closer as he pulsed into her mouth.

Then it happened. All hell broke loose as he came.

Estelle was unsure what exactly happened, but as he pumped his seed down her throat, he screamed, but no ordinary scream of ecstasy. This was mixed from man to—wolf.

He pushed her away roughly and she fell back on the bed dazed. Jack stood at the foot of the bed naked, but...he was convulsing.

"Jack! Jack, are you okay?" She tried to scramble over the bed to him but he moved away, his muscles shifting, increasing.

She sat mesmerized as Jack began to change. Hair burst out over his back, arms and legs. His body grew in mass—and shape.

He staggered toward the kitchen and she watched him become a thing of imagination and folklore.

Jack was a real werewolf.

* * * * *

He couldn't help it. Her sweet mouth sucking on his cock was too much to tolerate. The beast demanded release. Swaying on his feet in his apartment, his body shifted, transforming into his other self—a werewolf.

He didn't want to scare her. Fearing his hideous secret would lose her forever, he began to move to the window. *Escape into the night,* his human rationale said.

"Wait," her soft plea stopped him.

Jack didn't even want to turn around, to have her see his full wolfen form—a hybrid. On two legs and covered with hair, he was a real monster. No movie magic could come close to the full extent of his transformation.

"Don't leave me here, Jack."

"I told you I would change," he said in a deep growl-like voice.

"It's okay, Jack." He heard her move from the bed, her bare feet padding across the threadbare rug. "I'd love you no matter what."

"You can love a beast?" he asked incredulously.

"I can love you in any form." She placed a hand upon his shoulder and her warmth comforted him. "Love doesn't know conditions."

He turned his head to see her out the corner of his eye. "You are quick to accept me as a wolf. Why? Doesn't it frighten you?"

She softly pulled on his arm, forcing him to face her. "Jack, I will admit I am a bit scared of this. It isn't every day you meet a werewolf. But then, I always wanted a beast to love me. Maybe that is why I felt such a strong connection to you right off. Whatever the reason, I am not going to stop loving you because of this."

"I love you very much, Estelle. I have for a long time, ever since I saw you in the movies. I wanted so much to meet you." His large form towered over hers but she still fit perfectly to him. He drew her close into his arms. "Mel is a friend and he got me the job on the picture so I could meet you."

"Mel said I should march into the ISS offices and demand the gossip affair with Don is stopped."

"Damn right, you'll be on my arm from now on."

"No."

"No?"

"Only if you fuck me right now." She smiled and reached for his hand, pulling him to the bed.

"But... I'm—"

"A beast. My werewolf lover."

Chapter Five

ꙮ

Estelle loved him. It didn't matter what he was. She always said she wanted a beast to love her. She got her wish.

Okay, maybe she didn't think it would literally come true. But the attraction was there. Even now as he stood at the end of the bed, her cunt creamed with anticipation. His cock was enormous, erect and silently zeroing in.

She lay back on the bed and bent her knees. Letting her thighs fall open, she breathed, "Fuck me, Jack." He growled low and she reached down to spread her labia wider. Dipping a finger through her wetness, she entreated him further. "See, I am ready for you. I want you inside me, filling me, taking me."

Without a word, he climbed on the bed, the mattress giving under his weight. His arms braced his body over hers. He eased down over her and she groaned as his penis stroked along her slit.

She closed her eyes, but he commanded, "Keep them open. I want you to see what is making you feel pleasure."

"I see Jack."

"You see the wolf."

"Same thing."

"You're sure this doesn't bother you, my being…a monster?"

She moved her hips and coaxed his cock to enter her an inch. "I want you, however you look. I see beyond the appearance, I see the heart and soul of you, my Jack."

He sighed and pulled back from her opening then pushed forward. She cried out as he slowly entered her, filling her one agonizing inch at a time. Just when she thought he'd push in farther, completing his sensual torture, he pulled back, leaving her starving for more.

"Oh, Jack, why are you doing this to me?"

He paused his retreat. "Because I don't want to hurt you."

"You're not hurting me in a bad way. You're driving me crazy." She flexed her hips in her need. She demanded to have him, and if she had to—

That was it. He was afraid of hurting her. So guess what, she was going to take the reins of control.

"Get on your back."

He gazed down at her questioningly. "What?"

"I want to ride you."

"Mmm… I like that." It didn't take a second before he was on his back.

She straddled his body and enjoyed his massive build between her legs. She took his cock in one hand and guided it up inside her body.

"Fuck!" he cried as he arched his back.

She paused at the sheer joyous sensation of him filling her, his cock stretching her walls to the limit, pulsing with life deep within.

His hands upon her hips, he began to guide her as she moved up and down over him. Each time he penetrated her, she yelped with pleasure.

She wanted to ride him, pump over his length faster, and she grabbed the headboard for leverage as she increased the rhythm.

Riding his cock like she was a bitch in heat, she stopped thinking rationally. There was nothing more than here and now, her in bed with Jack, fucking him into a frenzy. Glancing down at his wolfen face, she saw how he fought to hold back just a little longer.

Lost within the throes of passion, the dam burst and she came. The room tilted, all the power and energy within zeroed in on her intimate connection with Jack. They were as one body, one heart. As her muscles squeezed and released, jolts of ecstasy shot through her every pore. She screamed with each contraction, milking out every last moment of pleasure.

Just when she thought she couldn't take any more, Jack moved. He slipped out of her channel and she almost cried at the loss.

"Don't worry, babe, I'll fill you up again." Only an edge of control laced his voice. He rose from the bed and Estelle fell forward, collapsing from her spent strength. "No, babe, we're not done."

He tugged on her hips, raising her ass into the air. On her knees, she leaned upon her elbows. He positioned her knees apart and she felt exposed. Creamy juice began to run down the inside of her thigh, and then she felt his tongue lick it away.

His tongue followed the wet trail upward to her cunt. Her strength began to come back as her body poised in anticipation.

When his tongue touched the puckered flesh of her anus, she jumped. It was oddly delightful and after a few slow passes, she was whimpering for more.

He stopped and she almost cried out in disappointment until she felt his finger test the entrance.

"Relax, babe. This is going to feel so good. I can fuck you so good back here and you'll come so hard, you'll beg for more."

She honestly didn't care just as long as he kept on touching her there. It was uncomfortable at first, but as he worked the muscles, they loosened as she relaxed. Now, she craved more.

Then he removed his finger and before she could complain, he slowly advanced into her hole.

"Oh—oh—"

Pain. Pain. "Oh—oh...oh my!" Pain turned into exquisite pleasure. His cock deeply inside her, he paused for her to grow accustomed to the size.

When he began to move within her, she was lost in ecstasy. Nothing felt so glorious. She never participated in anything so…taboo. Oh my! No wonder it was taboo, anything that felt so good had to be.

His pace quickened and she felt him surge with each thrust. He grasped her hips and pumped into her. His breathing became labored and his grip rough.

"Estelle!" he cried when he came.

Warm semen spurted up into her rear and it was all she could take. She climaxed right along with him. Such unparallel sensations. Desire, attraction, excitement, and love meshed together and surrounded them, binding them together as one.

She was his mate.

Spent, he retreated and his limp cock slipped from her. He lay down on the bed as she collapsed and turned onto her back. They lay there for several minutes catching their breaths.

Glancing over at him, she was shocked. Jack wasn't a wolf then, but his human self. "What happened?" she asked as she leaned her body against him, the warm touch of his moist skin a welcome sensation.

"Not sure. I changed just before I came. It was as though— as though the beast receded into my body."

"And the man took over." She stroked back a stray hair from his forehead.

"Pretty much." He turned to look at her, his eyes locking with hers, "Only my true mate can tame the beast."

"This mean I won't have him in bed anymore?" she chuckled.

"Oh no, I'm still a werewolf, but only you can tame my wild side."

"How about we save the *wild* for the bedroom, deal?"

"Only if you break that stupid contract deal about Don."

"Oh, blackmail is it?" When she saw he wasn't smiling she sobered. "You got a deal. We'll go in tomorrow and face off with the execs."

* * * * *

The next morning Jack went into the ISS office with Estelle. She demanded the publicity using her in a supposed affair with Don be ended. They weren't too enthusiastic with the change, claiming it was in her contract that they controlled her publicity and that of ISS.

"I don't care. You can't control my life." She stood her ground in front of the middle-aged ISS owner, Sylvester March.

"Besides, my wife can't go out with Don unless you want the gossip columns to really smear the studio in the mud." Jack was calm about his announcement.

In half of a heartbeat, Sylvester relented, then added, "I expect a picture starring you both for this change."

Jack shook the man's hand. "I don't see that as a problem, sir."

"You're a buff-looking guy. Ever do any acting not wearing a mask?"

"No sir."

"We'll take some tests but I think that you'll be perfect for our next production. Mel is going to direct that one."

"What's it called?" Estelle asked.

"*Werewolf in L.A.*"

* * * * *

"Who the fuck do you think you are?" Don stormed into her dressing room without knocking.

"What? Don, get out!"

121

He grabbed her by the shoulders from her vanity stool. "Think you can leave me out in the cold, little hussy? Think fucking a stuntman will get you far in this town?"

"Let go of me, you ass!" She struggled but in his anger, Don was incredibly strong.

"How about I soil the goods a bit for your new man? Bet he wouldn't want you after that."

"Let go—"

The door slammed open and Jack burst into the small room. Estelle recognized the beast controlling him, he must have heard Don yelling at her outside.

"Don!" Jack growled, and thrust the smaller man away.

Jack's emotions ran too high. The human side was losing grip. His body began to transform as he reached for the man's shirt, pulling Don away from her.

Don shook in horror as Jack grew larger before his eyes, his face altered, his canines lengthening.

Jack shoved Don out the door of the dressing room, and the man flew out and onto the ground. He shuffled to get up, but Jack was on him again.

"You get your filthy hands off my mate!" Jack was incensed. Lifting the man by his shirt once again, Jack pulled him closer, and snarled, "Next time you touch her, I will rip you limb from limb."

"Jack," she said in a quiet voice. "Jack."

Reluctantly he gazed up at her.

"Let him go, Jack. He won't bother us anymore."

"No! No, I won't bother her…or you. I will stay clear." Don was stammering. It was a pitiful display of weakness.

Jack leaned over Don's face and growled, "You're lucky she's here." He tossed Don from his grasp, and added, "Now get out."

Don's retreat was something Estelle took a secret joy in. The man was a snake and his constant reminding her that she was under contract to date him was finally at an end.

"Estelle." Jack sounded calmer now.

She smiled up at her hulk of a man. "Jack."

"I love you, Estelle."

"And I love you, too."

"Got time for a quickie in your dressing room?" he asked with a wink.

"I think with Don on the run, we may have time for more than a quickie."

He scooped her up into his arms and laughed. "Time for this beast to ravish his beautiful mate."

"Take me, you beast."

Also by Marianne LaCroix

ଛଠ

Beast In My Bed
Descendants of Darkness
Eternal Embrace
Lady Sheba

About the Author

ଛଠ

Multi-published author Marianne LaCroix lives in the American south in the land of cotton and mint juleps. She's an active member of the RWA in the ESPAN, GothRom, Passionate Ink, and First Coast Romance Writers chapters. She's had several recognitions for her writing including a *Romantic Times BOOKClub* Reviewer Choice nomination. Her tastes run to the alpha male with a dark streak in the form of a vampire, shape-shifter or other tortured-soul type. When not writing, Mari can be found with her twin toddler girls and her husband of eleven and half years.

Marianne welcomes comments from readers. You can find her website and email address on her author bio page at www.ellorascave.com.

PRIESTESS OF DESIRE

Mary Winter

Chapter One

ဢ

Heavy footsteps echoed in the hall outside. Daphine Shalwood failed to suppress the shudder of fear slithering down her spine. Closing her eyes, she recited an invocation to Zudiat, her Goddess, and reminded herself why she stood here, chained in the prince's bedchambers. The Rite of Completion, when she lost her maidenhead and completed her training as a priestess of Zudiat. As a member of the temple just a few blocks down from the king's palace, she should have given this honor to the king. She could handle him, with his salt-and-pepper hair and kind eyes. His firstborn, Sethe, however, made her think dark things, dangerous things that, should she speak of them, would get her expelled from her order.

Her shoulders ached. With her hands manacled over her head, she could only lean against the wall for support. Luckily, she didn't have to stand on tiptoe, and she didn't have to share this honor with anyone else. She had no other year mates. She shuddered, and not from fear.

The door creaked open. Daphine refused to see who entered. Servants came and went, seeing to her needs, but their steps didn't shake the room, didn't make heat coil in her womb. No, this would be Prince Sethe Cavelblood, heir to the Pyndaria throne. Daphine swallowed hard.

Two footsteps, then the door closed. She turned, helpless to resist the pull of him even across the room. Wearing dirty breeches, boots, and little else, Sethe stood just inside the door. His eyes traveled over her form, from the jut of her breasts against the white silk scarf binding them, to the matching triangle of fabric covering her sex, and every inch of flesh in between. She willed herself not to be moved by his hungry gaze. *I'm just completing my testing. That's why I'm chained here. For the ritual.* In spite of her mental words heat raced through her and her pussy clenched.

"My Lord." Daphine bowed her head, as much out of courtesy as to pull her gaze from the sight of his broad chest with its dusting of blond hair. She kept her head bowed as he neared, though she feared he'd hear the pounding of her heart. Her nipples tightened painfully under his regard, and she wondered how other priestesses had survived this night. None spoke of it, and she feared what might happen.

"Priestess." He cupped her chin, tilting her gaze up to meet his. "I regret they did not tell me you were here, otherwise I would have bathed."

An image of him lounging in a deep stone bath, his glorious body naked raced through her mind. He'd rise from the water, rivulets running over chiseled muscles to pool at his feet. One look, and she'd willingly lick him dry. Her cheeks heated at the direction of her thoughts. She had to quit thinking such things. Once this night ended she'd return to her temple, and the rest of her life she'd enjoy only the attentions of her fellow priestesses. The Glorious Mother protected all, but only if she shunned the company of men.

"It is all right, My Lord. Your duties are pressing."

He smiled, revealing a dimple in his cheek. "Yes, Priestess, they are." Lightly he stroked her arms, easily reaching the cuffs on her wrists. His fingers slowly teased her tender flesh. Pleasure radiated from his touch, making her breasts heavy with need and her pussy moist. If this were just the beginning, she wondered how she'd survive the actual act itself. Even cloistered with other priestesses, she knew what happened between a man and a woman. Sacred scrolls told of the act, and she had to learn those scrolls before she came to this ritual.

Sethe leaned in close, his lips hovering next to her. His scent filled her nostrils, a heady mix of sweat and male musk. She fought against inhaling it deeper. Becoming attached to this man, any part of him, would doom her. Just forget she'd ever seen him about town. Just because she ran errands for the temple, her privilege as a higher priestess, and happened to long for a glimpse of the handsome prince didn't mean she pined for him like a maiden in a tale.

He licked her earlobe. "Mmm, you taste so good. Will you taste as good all over?"

Daphine shuddered. Nowhere in the scrolls did it say how delicious a man's touch felt.

His lips skimmed the column of her throat and ignited a trail of fire in her body. Not even the tentative touches she gave herself caused this much pleasure. His breath, warm and moist, floated over her skin. The folds of her sex plumped with desire, and a trickle of moisture escaped. Great Goddess, he had her so hot, so fast. She feared she might burn. His hands continued their maddening stroking of her arms.

Daphine fought against thrashing against her bonds. Her breasts ached for attention, and she rubbed them against his chest. A low chuckle erupted as his lips stilled just above the white fabric binding them. His fingers slid down her arms, behind her back, and quick tugs sent her scarves floating to the floor.

Sethe stepped back. His gaze zeroed in on her naked breasts. The hunger in his eyes shook her, made her want to feel his lips, his fingers, anything against the sensitive tips. "Please," Daphine whimpered.

"Please what?"

"Touch me." Her husky voice shocked her. She hastily added, "My Lord."

"As you command." He didn't touch her, not immediately. Instead, he caressed her sides, drawing tiny shivers from her. His thumbs brushed the sides of her breasts.

Daphine moaned. With arms and legs manacled, she could do nothing but arch against him, demanding he touch her. The heat in her cunt burned her, her desire a steady ache throughout her body. At last, he brushed a thumb against her nipple. Daphine arched, strung tight like a bow. Her body vibrated with the pleasure. Her breath caught, only to be expelled as a low moan as his lips closed around her hardened nipple.

Sethe toyed with her nipple, swirling his tongue around it, then licking it softly. He'd suck hard for a moment, the tug darting all the way to her pussy, then release it to blow gently against her heated skin. The chill breeze only made her want more. Daphine forced herself to remain still. Thrashing in her bonds would only dislodge the heavenly mouth attached to her nipple. Sethe used his other hand to squeeze and massage her breast.

Moisture flooded her pussy. She could feel it, hot and slick, waiting for the silky length of Sethe's cock. Her tiny whimpers turned into heavy moans as he rubbed his hard cock against her. Even through his breeches, she felt his swollen length and knew he wanted her too.

Sethe pulled back. He stared into her eyes. "Are you ready?"

Daphine wanted to scream with frustration. Was she ready? Did he not smell her arousal in the air? Did he not feel the drop of moisture sliding down her thighs? "Please My Lord, take me." She trembled.

He soothed her with a touch, his hands so light against her flesh she thought she might have imagined them. Dropping to his knees before her, he rained tiny kisses between her breasts, then lower as he marked a trail to where she wanted him the most. A quick nudge on the inside of her thighs had her widening them as much as she could against her restraints.

He drew a line along her labia with his finger, a quick caress that left her hungry for more.

"My Lord, you're tormenting me." He slid a finger into her up to the first knuckle, pulling a moan from her. A stroke across her clit, once, twice, and she shuddered, so close to orgasm she could feel herself straining over the precipice.

Then he kissed her. His lips wrapped around her clit, drawing it deep into his mouth like a ripe berry.

Daphine screamed. Pleasure broke over her in waves. Her body pulsed, and all the while, Sethe remained fastened to her clit, driving her orgasm. A flick of his tongue, and she shuddered again.

At last she stilled against his seeking mouth. She glanced down at him kneeling between her legs. Never in her life had she seen a more beautiful image. Her temple pictured her Goddess lounging with naked women catering to her, but never had she seen a man kneel in supplication at a woman's pussy. Looking down on his dark blond hair highlighted to gold by the sun, his broad tanned shoulders, Daphine worked to catch her breath. He looked, she thought, like the God come to life. And if her Goddess had this pleasure, then why would she turn away? A shiver darted down her spine.

Sethe stroked her. His fingers slid easily into her, and he slowly filled her aching channel with two of his digits.

Daphine's eyelids fluttered closed. Slowly, Sethe finger-fucked her, his thumb brushing against her clit with every stroke. Her inner walls tightened.

Knowledge. As part of her training, she had to learn the joining of male and female. Just this once, before she sequestered herself in the temple. Sethe's gentle fingers barely breeched her, yet as he added a third, she wondered what his cock would feel like sliding into her. Heaven, most likely, of a kind reserved only for those honored by the Goddess.

Sethe stood. His fingers slid from her, their absence a loss. Daphine clenched her muscles around him, wanting to hold any part of him inside. Instead, he stepped back and quickly unfastened his breeches. He toed off his boots. They joined his breeches in a puddle on the floor.

Daphine stared. Prince Sethe looked magnificent. In her maiden's ways, she could find no words to describe him except godlike. He stood, body honed and muscular from fighting alongside his father's soldiers. His cock rose like a flagpole from his loins, thick and hard. The head emerged from the skin surrounding it, and Daphine licked her lips. She wanted to taste him. "My Lord," she gasped. With his girth, he'd fill her, his thick length invading her body. The priestesses never told her this part of her training would be so delicious.

"I'll be careful." Sethe stepped forward. He paused before her and she saw his throat bob as he swallowed.

Almost reverently, he cupped her breasts. His thumbs played with her nipples, drawing them into even tighter peaks. "I'll try not to hurt you, Priestess, but the first time always comes with a bit of pain. Just relax." He rubbed his cock against her. It slid easily against her slick pussy.

The delightful friction rubbed against her clit. Daphine thought she might come again, then he paused, his head poised at her opening. Sethe's hands stilled. His gaze caught hers, hungry and insistent, but at the same time unsure.

Did he fear she might not accept him? Not when her desire hummed in her veins like the finest wine. He entered her with a long, sure stroke.

Daphine keened her pleasure. Leaning forward, Sethe captured her lips with his. His tongue delved into her open mouth, his hands curved around her breasts, fingers pinching her nipples. Sethe thrust forward. A brief flare of pain, muffled by the hands on her breasts and the tongue in her mouth. Then, pleasure, pure heavenly pleasure as Sethe buried himself balls-deep inside her. She swallowed his moan. Daphine hung in her bonds, the thick cock buried so deep inside her she didn't know where Sethe ended and she began.

He started to withdraw. Slow, so annoyingly slow, she wanted him to fuck her hard into oblivion. Her muscles milked him, stretched around him as he pulled away. Restraint throbbed in every muscle of his body. Daphine wiggled on his cock. She didn't want it slow. Not now. Not with the experience of being filled. She wanted to be impaled on him until she came in a screaming climax.

Sethe thrust forward again. Over and over he thrust into her body, each stroke harder and deeper than the first. Daphine hung on. She fisted her hands even as her pussy fisted around his cock. Just a little more. Just a little higher. Then she screamed. Pleasure radiated through her body. "Yes! Goddess yes!" she yelled.

Sethe growled. His hands lowered to her waist, held her still for his pistoning cock. One thrust. Two. Then he stiffened inside her. Veins stood out on his neck, his body rigid inside hers. His hot seed splashed her insides. The force of his climax wrung another one from Daphine, and she shrieked her pleasure to the world.

He remained inside her for long moments, his breath coming in harsh pants. Daphine realized her breathing matched his, and found she couldn't be ashamed of her wanton behavior. On the contrary, she wanted more of it. Yet she'd return to her temple and never see Prince Sethe Cavelbood again. The thought filled her with an aching sadness.

Sethe exhaled a long sigh, then brushed his lips across her forehead. "I hope I wasn't too rough." His fingers stroked her sweat-slick skin.

"Not at all, My Lord. You were perfect."

"As were you, my dear Priestess. As were you." His half-erect cock slid from her. He stepped away long enough to grab the key to her shackles and then unfastened the bands around her wrists and ankles. She fell against him, arms twining around his neck. Her fingers tingled. The pins and needles sensation didn't dampen the effect of being held against his broad chest. Carrying her over to the bed, he laid her down then sat beside her. "The feeling should return in a moment. I'm sorry you were shackled for so long, but the ritual required it." He massaged her hands and fingers until the feeling returned. "Wait here." He covered her with a soft down blanket.

Turning from the bed, he scooped up his breeches and pulled on a cord by the door. Moments later a servant appeared, and her prince gave the order for warm towels, a basin of water and for the tub to be filled with warm water. No sooner had the servants left, than he returned to her side.

Daphine didn't know what to expect, but it wasn't for the prince to start making orders for her comfort. She nibbled on her lower lip, unsure how to act. Once the ritual was completed, and she had no doubt it had been, she expected to return to the temple.

A servant knocked on the door. Sethe let the young men in with buckets of water, and accepted a small basin and warm clothes from them. Watching him carry them back to the bed, Daphine wondered how to broach the topic of getting back to the temple. Her duties called to her now that the ritual was completed. Being here with the prince only tested her resolve.

His broad chest caught her gaze, and her fingers curled with the need to reach out and touch him. As soon as the servants finished bringing water for the bathtub, a surprisingly quick process, he folded the blanket aside. "Let me clean you up." He wrung out the cloth in the basin and started washing the insides of her thighs.

"You don't have to do that, my pri— My Lord." She'd almost called him "my prince." He wasn't hers. He belonged to the entire kingdom, and after tonight, she'd never experience such intimacy with him, or any other man, again.

"Yes I do." He nudged her thighs wider apart and brushed the warm rag against her labia.

Daphine closed her eyes. A soft moan emerged from her throat. "That feels—"

"Good?" Sethe's eyes twinkled with humor. "I hope so, Priestess."

"Daphine, please." His gentle ministrations wound them in a cocoon of intimacy. As soon as he cleaned her, he scooped her up and carried her into the bathing room. Daphine marveled at the tub large enough for two hewn from local stone. She hadn't paid attention to the servants filling it, but to think of them going to all that trouble for her, a lowly priestess of Zudiat, filled her with a sense of awe.

"Your bath, Daphine." Gently, he lowered her into the tub

and then reached for the waistband of his trousers. Fabric fell and he stood gloriously naked, so close she could reach out and touch him.

She hadn't a chance to explore chained to the wall, and if she only had tonight she didn't want to miss the opportunity. Rising onto her knees, she leaned over the edge of the tub. Cool stone chilled her breasts, and her nipples hardened into tiny nubs. Splaying her hands across his abdomen, she traced each line and ridge of his rippled abdomen. Up to where her fingers grazed his male nipples, then lower to the springy hair surrounding his cock, she stroked.

Sethe's sharp inhalation filled the room.

Daphine cradled his cock in her fingers. She stroked it, satiny smooth skin over a core of steel. From base to tip, pausing to tease the tiny slit in the end, she caressed his cock. With her other hand, she fondled his balls. A tiny pearl of fluid leaked out his tip, and she leaned forward and licked it away.

"Priestess," he groaned. "Goddess bless."

His words reminded Daphine of her calling, of her vows she'd be taking now that the ritual was complete. But for tonight, the Goddess had given her to him. Surely Zudiat would bless this coupling as well as the other one, for tonight was to have her intimately know a man before taking her vows. She pulled back and looked up at him, a soft smile on her face. "Yes, the Goddess does bless." Before he could do anything, she leaned forward and wrapped her lips around him.

Daphine drew him into her mouth, her pussy clenching. She started slowly, licking and suckling him until she could take him completely into her mouth. Her cheeks hollowed out as she sucked.

Sethe threaded his fingers in her hair, holding her in place. Gently he fucked her mouth, his groans and growls of desire heating up her blood. She made him do this. Daphine, priestess to Zudiat and barely tried maiden, made Prince Cavelblood's cock hard. Power rushed through her, far headier than any she'd known in her ecclesiastic studies. Reaching around him, she grabbed his ass and kneaded gently.

He tasted salty and full of promise. In the water, her clit swelled, pussy aching for something, anything to fill it. With her nipples against the cool edge of the tub, the contrast of hot and cold rolled through her like a shock. Sethe bit back a cry and pushed her away.

"My Lord?" she queried, afraid she might have done something wrong.

Sethe knelt by the tub and ran his thumb along her full lower lip. "Fear not, you were doing everything right. But this night is your ritual. This night is for you." With those words, he picked up a rag and a bar of spiced soap and started to bathe her skin.

Daphine relaxed under his ministrations. She glanced down at his erect cock and hoped she'd get to experience it once more before the night ended.

* * * * *

Daphine blinked her eyes against the glare of sunlight filtering through the temple's stained glass windows. Her knees ached from kneeling on the stone floor since midnight, praying at the altar of Zudiat. Swallowing hard, she listened to the familiar sounds of bells ringing first prayers and the chatter of novices as they filled into the temple proper. Daphine lurched to her feet. She braced herself with one hand on the marble base of the statue, then she tottered off to the private meditation room. Even after spending the rest of the night on the stone floor of the temple with the night breezes chilling her to the bone, she still thought of Sethe.

Even now an image of him rose in her mind, his long fingers stroking her skin to fevered pitch. The heavy weight of her breasts filled his hands perfectly, as if they'd been made for each other. Daphine shook her head. Now that she'd passed her training such thoughts were unseemly for a priestess. She stared at the golden statue of Zudiat in the corner of the room with several candles lit around its base and knelt. Bowing her head, she prayed for forgiveness. The scent of patchouli filled the air, and Daphine hoped the smoke would carry her plea to the Goddess.

Her shoulders ached, a muscle jumping between her shoulder blades. She longed to rise and work out the kinks in her muscles. She wouldn't. The Goddess sent the pain as her punishment.

Daphine traced the feet of the statue with a gentle caress, noticing the patina of the bronze from the caress of many hands over the years. "Oh Great Mother, why did it have to be the prince who completed my training? I've held an irreverent fascination for him since I saw him at his first tournament. His father I could have handled and returned here pure of heart. But now, all I can think about is Sethe. His hands, his lips, even his cock, Great Mother. I know you spurned the High Father and your abstinence has brought us these times of plenty. I fear I lack your strength." She bowed her head once more and started to recite the first of the twelve prayers of holiness.

The door creaked open. Daphine remained kneeling. Perhaps a novice needed some time to contemplate the life she was about to choose. Often she had shared this room with her fellow priestesses in silent, private prayer.

"Daphine." The High Priestess' voice filled the room. "I thought I might find you here."

Daphine looked up from her prayers to see the woman who had taken her in standing in the doorway. Although age streaked her long black hair with gray, and a few more lines bracketed her face, High Priestess Solindari looked nearly the same as she had all those years ago. "High Priestess." Daphine knelt forward and pressed her head to the floor. Her back and knees protested the movement.

"Rise, my child. You did not join the others for breakfast. First prayers have ended and still you pray? Did things go badly with the ritual?" Folding her lavender skirts around her,

Solindari sat on one of the plush benches. She patted the seat next to her. "Join me."

Daphine obeyed. "Thank you, High Priestess. The ritual went well." She felt the red flush of heat creep over her cheeks and down her throat.

"Maybe too well, my child?"

Daphine blushed even harder. "Yes." She hung her head in shame.

"And now your thoughts are filled with the young man. Am I correct?"

Daphine nodded.

"Do not despair, my dear. The fact you've been praying all night shows me you're ready for your vows. They will happen on the next full moon as planned. Do you think you're the only priestess who has second thoughts after she experiences the pleasures of the flesh? It is why the ritual was created. If you pass that and lose your maidenhead and can still face the Goddess in the morning, then you're ready for your vocation." Solindari patted Daphine's knee. "You'll see in time." She rose to her feet and started for the door. "Why don't you go down to the kitchens for a light repast and meet me in the library. We have much to do before the next full moon." Without waiting for an answer, she turned and left.

Daphine stared at the closed door. Could it really be? Did the High Priestess still think her worthy of vows? Taking a deep breath, she squared her shoulders, and with a last, lingering look at the Goddess' statue followed her High Priestess out the door.

* * * * *

Sethe darted nimbly away as the sword passed close enough to his side to ruffle his tunic. Damn it, that had been a close one. He held his sword in a defensive position and stared at one of his many cousins, Havlinar. He moved back, his dark brown hair disheveled. Sweat plastered his tunic to him, and Sethe plucked at his own soaked clothing. "One more time all right?"

Havlinar nodded. "All right, but I might get you this time."

Sethe chuckled with far more bravado than he really felt. Usually he trounced his slightly younger cousin, but this morning his mind had been elsewhere—like back in his bedroom with the tempting young priestess. She stirred his blood like none of the cows his mother had thrown at him in the hopes of securing a stable heir to the throne. With relatives ruling most of the countries on the eastern continent, prospects for a suitable marriage partner were slim, and growing slimmer with each woman he dismissed. His mother's joke about looking to the daughters of the stable hands wasn't far off. But none of them stirred him like the priestess.

Sethe shook his head as Havlinar took advantage of his momentary lapse. The clash of steel filled the air, a satisfying counterpoint to the grunts of exertion. With the sun beating down and a good battle before him, Sethe tried to turn his mind to his duty rather than his desire.

Chapter Two

❧

Tucking the basket under her arm, Daphine hurried through the crowded market. The potter promised the temple some new oil urns, and the High Priestess asked Daphine to check with him as she ran her errands. The aromas of fresh baked goods, roasting meat and animals filled the air. She passed a perfume seller, the cloying aromas nearly making her gag. Half a dozen lower noble ladies gathered around the booth, all chattering or bartering over some trinket or another.

A flash of jealousy darted through her. These were the kind of ladies Sethe would wed. Not the lowly daughter of a blacksmith turned priestess. She shook her head. Thoughts of marriage were futile. After all, she devoted her body and her life to the Goddess.

As if thoughts of Sethe conjured him up, he stood two booths down from her. He held a leather scabbard in his hands and turned it over, looking at the craftsmanship. Daphine slipped into an empty spot next to the candlemaker's tent.

"Priestess. So good to see you." The old woman reached beneath the cloth covering the table and pulled out four sweet beeswax candles. "For the temple. Please, take them with my blessing."

Trying to keep an eye on Sethe, she slipped the candles into her basket. "Thank you," she said with a bow of her head. "The High Priestess will be pleased with your generosity."

Sethe handed the scabbard back to the seller, then turned to leave.

"If you'll excuse me," Daphine said, ducking away as a woman stepped into her place at the candlemaker's booth.

Daphine started down the street, her gaze fixed on Sethe's

broad back. Today he wore a forest green tunic belted at the waist, and fine, black trews tucked into knee-length boots. He paused at the silversmith's booth and started to look. Daphine followed, thinking she could use the pretense of getting a new ritual chalice to cover her unnatural interest in the young prince.

She paused one seller down, looking at the leather goods with a disinterested eye. The seller watched her from back in his booth, certain a priestess had no use for scabbards and belts. A small pouch designed with a horse caught her eye, and she picked it up. Her father would love it for his belt, and she could send it home as a reminder of her existence. "How much is this?" she asked.

"Five crowns."

Daphine's face fell. She set the piece back with a small shake of her head. Her monthly allowance granted her less than a crown, certainly far less than the leatherworker would haggle. "Thank you," she said and turned toward the silversmith.

Sethe appeared in deep discussion with the man over a pair of tankards set before him.

Daphine started toward the seller.

A cart barreled down the road. The crowd parted. Someone jostled Daphine, sending her stumbling forward. She tried to catch herself. Her slipper caught. Stumbling, she tried to right herself. Around her, the crowd milled and shoved one another as the cart loomed near. The clatter of wheels against cobblestones and the pounding of hooves filled the air. Someone shoved her. Her basket tipped, the candles spilling over the ground and breaking.

Sethe's green coat wavered in her vision. He turned, and she feared stumbling into him. *Oh no, don't let me see him. Not after the ritual.* Then one arm snaked around her and she found herself pulled against a hard, muscular chest.

"Easy, I've got you." The deep voice filled her head and turned her knees to jelly.

Daphine grabbed the arm of his coat, looking around to try

and step away. Only the arm holding her tightened. She blinked, suddenly realizing Sethe held her. Oh Goddess!

The cart rushed past, so close wind of its passage ruffled her hair.

Daphine started to back way.

The arm around her waist tightened, and her breasts flattened against his chest. Even through her cloak and gown her nipples hardened with the contact. She swore she felt the ridge of his cock pressing against her stomach. "Sir," she said. "My Lord. Please unhand me."

Her eyes widened when she realized the shopkeeper leered at her, as did several of the villagers nearby.

Sethe's hand moved from her back to her buttocks, squeezing gently. "If you wish." The playful grin on his face said he knew she wished no such thing.

Heat rushed to her cheeks. She wanted to reprimand him, not only as a priestess, but as a woman for his brazen behavior. Instead she pushed against his chest with her free hand. Hard muscles met her hand, and she longed to curl her fingers into his shirt. Instead, she shoved against him. "My Lord. Let go of me this instant! I am a Priestess of Zudiat."

In the crowd, people gasped.

"My Lord Prince, you best be letting her go," the shopkeeper said.

Slowly, Sethe released the arm around her waist. "I wish I could do more than hold you, Priestess," he whispered in her ear.

The words shook her. If the crowd hadn't pressed around them, she feared she might have fallen. As it was, she turned and looked at the silversmith's wares, hoping to find distraction from the handsome man. Her gaze fell on an elaborately decorated knife. The tiger-shaped hilt boasted real tiger's-eye stones for eyes. Each intricately carved paw rested on a pearl. The weapon came with its own matching silver scabbard.

"Thinking of killing me?" Sethe asked in her ear.

"I wouldn't dream of it, My Lord," she replied with a saccharine smile on her face. Daphine leaned in closer, and whispered into his ear, "But if you make another public display like the last one, I could use it to turn you into a temple eunuch."

Sethe blanched.

She turned her attention to the silversmith. "Your work is beautiful. I shall recommend it to my High Priestess." Without waiting for a reply from the prince, she turned and strolled back through the market, happy to have gotten the best of the infuriating prince.

* * * * *

The cloying smell of perfume teased his nose and made it itch. Sitting in his mother's parlor, he faced the queen of the realm. Although gray streaked her blonde hair and bearing five children had thickened her waist, she still looked regal and beautiful. Her ladies, usually following her like goslings after a goose, were conspicuously absent.

Sethe's stomach churned. Not another one of these damned meetings with his mother. He wondered when she'd realize he was a grown man and not subject to her rule anymore. She might have dictated his life as a child, but now he had his own desires, and they had nothing to do with any of the young, and not so young, women she threw at him on a weekly basis. With the king away on business, she used her husband's absence to step up her campaign to get him married.

Sethe watched her place a few more stitches on her embroidery, still not acknowledging his presence. "I'm not marrying her."

Queen Rosalyn looked at her son and pursed her lips. "You don't even know who she is, dear. I have it on good authority that she's—"

Sethe held up his hand, silencing his mother. "I've heard it all before. How many is this? Twenty? Thirty? Do you think those ladies like being paraded before me like the fatted calf? I will marry when I find someone I can love. Someone I want to be with, not just someone noble enough to be my consort."

Rosalyn sighed. "Sethe, you may be the oldest, but you always were the most fanciful. It's your father's fault. He raised you on the stories of nobles and knights." She laughed and sipped the water glass sitting next to her hand. "Love doesn't enter into a state marriage, my dear. How many times have I told you that?"

"But you love my father. You've said as much yourself." Sethe grinned, happy to have caught his mother in her own trap.

"But I grew to love him. I knew what was expected to me as a dutiful daughter, so I married him. I grew to love him in time. Love at first sight is for fairy tales. And if you won't marry, I know your younger brothers would be happy to find a consort and take over the throne."

Sethe hated the implied threat in his mother's voice. So they would disinherit him rather than let him follow his heart? His mother's mercenary nature chilled him. "Fine. I'll abdicate."

Rosalyn gasped. "What?"

"If you don't think I'm fit to be the heir, then I'll abdicate the throne. Become a sell sword or something. I'm certainly good enough with a sword, and you know if I abdicated I couldn't stay with the guard, not without suspicion. I won't give in to your plans. Either you let me chose my own consort, or I'll relinquish my position as heir. It's as simple as that." He rose to his feet and bowed. "Now, if you'll excuse me, I have things to do." Amid his mother's sputtering he turned and left the room. Only once he was well down the corridor did he allow a triumphant grin on his face. Let his mother put that in her hen and roast it. Thoughts of the young priestess filled his mind and hardened his cock. Now if only he could convince a certain young priestess she deserved more than chastity for the rest of her life.

* * * * *

144

The austere antechamber failed to dim Sethe's hopes. Just a chance to see Daphine before she took her vows and was lost to him forever. Hadn't he'd been told stories all his life about his grandfather, who not finding a suitable prospect, had taken a consort from the Zudiat priestesses. They blessed the wedding, and his actions averted a war. Looking at the mural of Zudiat offering food to the poor, Sethe wondered if Daphine might be his priestess bride.

The door opened. The High Priestess entered. Long white robes covered her, and a cord of golden thread tied the gowns at her waist. Her feet, as was the tradition of Zudiat, were bare. An aura of power surrounded her. She sat, hands folded in her lap. Her eyes held great wisdom and great faith.

"High Priestess." Sethe rose to his feet and bowed deeply. "I'm honored you agreed to meet with me."

"I do what I must to prevent harm to my priestesses." Her stern words dimmed his hope.

"Harm? I have no desire to harm any of your order. I ask-"

She held up her hand. "I know what you ask, My Lord. I'm afraid I cannot grant your request. As the moon turns, Daphine prepares to take her vows. I will not have her swayed from her course by a handsome man and a handful of petty promises. You will have to find a consort, and where will that leave Daphine? Soiled, unfit for the priestess, or any trade. This is all she's known. I will not turn her back to her family disgraced, and quite possibly with child, because you cannot control your urges. I suggest you go back to the castle and seek a far more suitable maid to be your plaything." She frowned.

Her harsh words cut Sethe. He expected resistance, yes, but to have the High Priestess speak to him in such a way infuriated him. "I'm sorry, High Priestess. I have no desire of harming Daphine in any way." He rose to his feet. "Thank you for your time."

"Do not think to defy me. Daphine will not be swayed from this course."

"Or will you not allow her to be swayed?" With that parting shot, he opened the door and stepped into the temple. Striding across the stone floor, he watched novices, some as young as five, file into the temple. He slipped up the stairs to the box reserved for royalty and sat. He'd see for himself whether Daphine wanted to take her vows or not.

* * * * *

Sethe waited until prayers finished, then made his way down from the royal box. Although the novice priestesses tried to concentrate on their worship, scattered whispers and giggles erupted. A stern priestess frowned at him as she ushered her young charges out of the temple. Had the High Priestess spoken of him, the young prince who wished to steal one of their own away? Sethe hoped so. He glanced at the statue of Zudiat standing dour-faced over her worshippers. He believed in a dual deity, one in which the God was matched by an equally powerful Goddess. Though he understood why Zudiat turned away from men, Sethe wished she wouldn't ask the same of her priestesses.

Daphine brought up the rear, lagging behind. Watching her, Sethe wondered if she knew he stood there waiting. For a moment he thought not, for she nearly passed him. She stopped and faced him.

"My Lord." Daphine risked glancing toward the backs of the departing priestesses, then back into the chapel. She squared her shoulders and took a step away, putting distance between them. "You desire to worship Zudiat this morning?" She arched an eyebrow.

The stern Goddess standing watch over them failed to dampen his desire for Daphine. Sethe's cock twitched. "I could spend hours worshipping the perfection of your flesh, but I don't think that's what the Goddess had in mind."

Her cheeks flushed.

Sethe stepped forward. He clasped her hand, twining her

fingers with his to keep her from fleeing. "Can we talk?" Three closed doors lined the far edge of the chapel. He hoped one of them led to a private room. Though the statue of the Goddess didn't quell his ardor, neither did it inspire him to the words he knew he must say.

Daphine's small, pink tongue darted out to lick her lower lip. Sethe tried not to groan with frustration. She glanced back toward the doors, then around the temple. "There are private rooms over there." She gestured to the three doors with her free hand.

Sethe fought the urge to pull her close and wrap his arms around her. Instead, he nodded. "All right. Take us there."

Trepidation radiated from Daphine in waves. She kept glancing around, even up at the statue, as if she might be spotted. The High Priestess' words filled his mind, and Sethe wondered if the older woman had spoken so harshly to Daphine. He fought against the anger threatening to rise inside him. Daphine deserved free will, not to have her life dictated by a woman who shielded herself from life. It pained him to think of Daphine stuck in this temple, away from the villagers, him, forever. Her breathy cries echoed in his memory. The way her slick pussy fisted around his cock nearly drove him to hurry her into the room so he could take her up against the wall. A woman as passionate as her shouldn't be kept away from life. Not like this. Not against her will.

Daphine led them into the room and closed the door. A low couch sat along one wall. Murals depicting various scenes from Zudiat's life covered the walls. In once picture she passed out bread to the poor. In another, she blessed a young infant. Fertile fields and full bellies came from the cycle of life. From where else did infants come if they didn't start as the seeds of love planted in passion? Sethe sat on the low couch and stretched his legs before him.

Daphine released her fingers from his and stepped backward until she nearly crossed the small room. "Why did you come here?" Her taut nipples pressed against the fabric of the robe, and she fisted her hands in it, as if to keep from reaching for him.

"To see you."

"You've seen me. Now go away." She looked back toward the door, but didn't move.

Sethe rose to his feet. Across from him Daphine trembled like a newborn fawn. He crossed the two steps to reach her. "You're shaking. Of what do you have to be afraid?" Reaching out, he wrapped his arms around her.

In spite of her reluctance, she leaned against him. Her breasts, with their diamond-hard nipples, flattened against her chest. Her soft stomach against his hard cock nearly undid him. Biting his lip, he forced himself to be gentle, not to press her against the wall and fuck her over the picture of her Goddess. She burrowed into his warmth. Tentatively, her arms wrapped around him. "Of myself."

He nearly missed her soft whisper. He cupped her chin with his fingers and tilted her face so she looked at him. "Why are you afraid of yourself? Why can't you just let things happen between us?" He brushed his lips across hers, and even that brief taste heated his blood. "You haven't taken vows yet."

"But I will." She sighed, and her eyelids fluttered closed. "I came to the temple so sure of my vocation, so determined to serve the Goddess. And now, in your arms, I want to throw that all away. For what? You'll find a consort, and I'll be a defiled priestess." She shook her head. "I won't do it. I can't do it."

The pain in her words tore at him. Like him, she found herself trapped by other people's expectations. "But right now we can pretend. I'm not a prince, and you're not a priestess." He stepped forward, pressing her against the wall. "I want to be inside you so badly I ache."

Her breath hitched at his words.

"Would you like that? To have me inside you."

She nodded.

Sethe kissed her. Hunger built as he plundered her lips. He

swallowed her breathy cry, his tongue delving into her mouth. She returned the kiss, fingers clenching on his shoulders, mouth open beneath his. Her tongue stroked his, drawing it deeper into her mouth until she sucked on it.

Sethe fought for control. His cock pounded. Sliding his hand down her neck and shoulder, he cupped one breast in his hand. The nipple pressed against his thumb, and he stroked it, the peak hardening with a stroke of his fingers. Her hips moved against him. He couldn't wait. He should slow down, show her how wonderful it could be, but the rush of blood in his veins wouldn't let him. He wanted her now.

He slid his other hand beneath her ass, helping her lift one leg around his waist. Daphine needed no encouragement. She wrapped both legs around his waist. Sethe pulled his lips away long enough to whisper in her ear. "Hang on." He held her tight against him as he turned and crossed the room to the low couch. Sitting, he draped her over his chest so she straddled him. His hand palmed her ass.

Daphine pulled off her robe. She wore nothing underneath, and his mouth went dry. How could the Goddess not grant them the right to share in the beauty of each other's bodies? It seemed blasphemous not to. His fingers slid between her legs to her wet, swollen labia. She shuddered, biting off a cry as he slid a finger inside to stroke her clit. With his other hand, he unfastened his trousers.

There wasn't time to remove shirt or boots. His cock sprang eagerly through the opening. Sethe thrust two fingers inside her and stroked. God, she was so responsive, so beautiful. Her hips bucked. She swallowed her cries, not wanting them to be heard beyond the walls of the room.

"Please," she whispered. Her hands clutched at him, fisting in his shirt to stroke him through the fabric. Daphine caressed his cheeks, then slid her fingers into his hair, pulling his head toward her breast. "Please, Sethe, please."

The use of his first name shook him. Grabbing her hips, he held her poised above his cock. A drop of fluid leaked out the tip, and he clenched his teeth to keep from taking her like a wild animal. Leaning forward, he latched on to a hard nipple and sucked as he lowered her onto his cock.

By the gods, she felt good, her pussy clenching his organ as he slid deeper into her.

Daphine braced her hands on his shoulder, trying to move. His hands on her waist kept her still long enough for him to press balls-deep into her. He sat there for a moment, sucking hard on a nipple. She clenched her hands on his shoulder, her pussy milking him. She was close—so close—to orgasm. He dipped a finger between her legs and pressed her clit.

Daphine came with a shriek. She shuddered around him, her violent spasms shaking him. It took all his control not to surge upward, taking himself with her. Instead, he watched as she came on him. Her juices soaked his trousers. At last he could take no more. Turning his attention to her other breast, he grabbed her hips and thrust.

She bounced on his cock, eager in spite of her release. He fucked her, desperate to come inside her body. His balls drew tight against his body. The familiar tingling began in the base of his spine, and he stiffened. A roar of triumph threatened to break lose and he captured her lips, forcing her to swallow his cry of release. His cock pumped warm seed into her body, and he held her tight, buried deep within her, and never wanted to let go.

At last, he loosened his hold and leaned against the arm of the couch. Looking up at Daphine, he thought he never saw a more beautiful woman in his life. Her hair hung in disarray around her face, and a rosy glow covered her flesh. A small love bite began on her breast where he nipped her. His cock lay still half hard inside her.

Daphine glanced down at him and swallowed hard. Slowly, she stepped away, grabbing at the wall for a few moments until she retrieved her robe and covered herself. "I won't throw my vows away without a place to go. I will not dishonor my father," she said. "I'm sorry, Sethe, my prince. I'm sorry." She glanced up at the picture of the Goddess, and with the sheen of tears in her eyes, hurried out of the room.

Sethe stared at the closed door and wondered how to convince her to become his queen.

Chapter Three

ಐ

Sitting in the masculine confines of his father's war room, Sethe felt completely at ease. He leaned back in the leather chair and stretched his legs in front of him, crossing them at the ankles. Various maps sat scattered on a teak table between the two men, a half-empty bottle of watered wine and two empty goblets sitting on top of reports. Returned from his trip, his father, the king, sat beside him.

"I hear you're defying your mother again," he said, a grin on his face. "You know you're going to have to marry soon. I won't have talk of you abdicating your position as heir."

The humor in his father's voice gave way to a stern order. "I know. And I've found someone."

"Really? And your mother doesn't know." The king poured himself another glass of watered wine. He sipped. "Who is she?"

"A Zudiat priestess. Actually, it was a blessing you were away on your trip. I wouldn't have met her otherwise."

The king sucked in a harsh breath. "Do you know what you're doing, son? Be careful."

"My grandfather married a Zudiat priestess. I'm sure—"

"Your grandfather did what he had to do to end a war. You need to do no such thing, and I can't see why you would anger the temple with something so foolish. There are many women out there, a number of whom would make valuable allies and consorts." He frowned.

"And none of whom I like." Sethe sighed and leaned back. Of his parents, he expected his father to understand.

"Does she agree to be your bride?"

"I haven't asked her." Sethe picked up the empty glass and

stared into its depths. "I don't know."

"Ask her. Then we'll deal with the consequences." His father picked up the voluminous stack of reports.

Sethe knew a dismissal when he saw it. "Thank you," he said as he rose to his feet. He walked out of his father's war room feeling far brighter than he had in days.

* * * * *

Kneeling before her High Priestess, Daphine kept her gaze focused on the floor. Tapestries shrouded the stone walls of the High Priestess' personal chamber, each one depicting one of the stories of Zudiat's life. Daphine tried not to think upon the tapestries, this chamber, all of which might be hers if she stayed in the order. *My father might have been proud of me to be selected as a priestess, but surely he wouldn't want me to stay where I'm not happy.* After meeting Sethe, Daphine knew she'd never be happy cloistered within these walls.

"Rise, Daphine. You're nearly a full priestess. There's no need for you to act like a young novice," Solindari said.

Daphine saw the smile on the High Priestess' face and her heart fell. "There's something I need to tell you." She forced her voice to remain steady. "I will not be taking vows. I cannot enter into Zudiat's service."

Solindari nodded. "I expected as much, Daphine." She rose to her feet and rested a hand on Daphine's shoulder. "The Goddess does not take those unwilling to make the sacrifices. Your honesty is most appreciated. Are you sure?"

Daphine nodded. "Yes. I am sure." Just saying the words imbued her with strength. She wanted to shout her decision from the parapets, race to the castle and beg to see the prince.

"You will leave the temple with what you arrived with, yourself. We will provide one traveling robe, which is what you are wearing. Go in peace and may the Goddess bless you."

The finality of the High Priestess' words should have bothered her. Instead, they freed her. "Thank you." She turned and left Solindari's rooms with her head held high. In the corridor she passed no one as she made her way to the central temple.

The tapestries on the walls failed to move her as they had when she was younger. Instead, she saw them as scenes from a life she wouldn't live. A draft chilled her feet as she crossed the stone floor, and the scent of incense itched her nose. She ached to be outside, to be with Sethe again, with nothing between them.

She hurried into the central temple. Two novices, both too young to have their monthly courses, knelt before the temple, lips moving fervently in prayer. There would be others. Her own years raised in the temple's care seemed so long away now it seemed strange that she might have been so young, and so devoted as these young girls. They didn't look up from their prayers, and Daphine hurried past, anxious to be outside the temple. Her newfound freedom called to her, and she couldn't wait to see the prince.

*   *   *   *   *

A familiar figure walked up the flagstone path leading to the temple doors. Daphine rushed to the gate, her smile bright enough to rival the sun. Her robe whipped around her ankles and she grabbed it and pulled it above her knees so she could run easier. Sethe stopped. He stood there, staring at the closed gate. An emerald cloak tied at one shoulder hung behind him. In dress boots and a uniform, he cut a handsome figure and people stopped to stare.

Daphine flung open the gate and passed through, heedless of the iron hasp clanking back into place.

Sethe remained still.

Daphine slowed, worry over riding the joy filling her. He didn't move, didn't say anything. She stumbled on the flagstones, her soft slippers better suited to the smooth temple floors than the street. She stopped. "My prince." She curtseyed low, letting the skirt of her robe fall into place. "I'm glad you're here."

"Priestess." He nodded, acknowledging her. "Is there somewhere we can talk?"

His curt manner worried her. Daphine pointed to a small barn off to the side, used to house the carriage before the High Priestess took it out. "We can go over there."

He gestured for her to lead the way, and she did so, her trepidation growing with each step. As she opened the door to the building, she checked to be sure they were alone. They were, and she led him to a wooden bench just inside. The heavy stable door closed behind them, leaving them in near dark.

Daphine sat.

Sethe took a seat next to her. Reaching for her, he tangled his fingers with hers. "There's something I have to tell you." He squeezed her hands gently, a reassuring gesture that was anything but.

Daphine nodded. "All right. What is it?" All her earlier joy fizzled in light of Sethe's solemn mood.

Sethe released one of her hands to caress her cheek. She turned toward the touch, her eyelids fluttering closed. "If I worried you, I'm sorry," he said. "I didn't want to do this out in public." Sethe slid from the bench and dropped to one knee.

Daphine's heart hammered in her chest. With his warm hands gripping hers, and down on one knee, all the romantic stories told to children came rushing back to her. The gallant prince. The sweet maiden. Surely he wouldn't ask for her hand. It wouldn't work. As much as she wanted it to, a prince destined to be king wouldn't marry a priestess, even a disgraced one such as herself.

"Daphine, I've searched this kingdom and others looking for the right woman to sit by my side and take the mantle of my consort. Highborn and low have vied for the claim. Yet none of them have captured my heart, my soul as you have. I love you, my Priestess of desire. I love you, Daphine. Will you be my consort and when I become king will you rule as queen beside me?"

Daphine's breath caught in her throat. For long moments she stared at Sethe, half afraid to believe what she had just heard. He looked at her, a nervous expectancy in his gaze that set her heart pounding in her chest. "Yes!" she said. "Oh thank the Goddess, YES!" She launched herself at him.

Sethe's hands wrapped around her waist. He pulled her down, sprawling her over his body. The ridge of his hard cock pressed against her stomach, his lips raining tiny kisses over her forehead, her cheeks, her closed eyelids, and finally her lips. His mouth settled on hers, and it felt like coming home. His tongue traced the seal of her lips, and she opened her mouth with a sigh.

Hungrily she kissed him, half afraid he might change his mind. Rocking, she shimmied so his erection pressed against her panties. She rubbed against him as moisture gathered in her pussy and dampened the soft fabric separating them. She never imagined he would propose, her prince, that he would make her his queen.

His tongue stroked hers, his hands tugging at her robe. She lifted her arms and he tossed the material aside. One tug on her panties and the material ripped. Naked, she straddled him, her hands just as eager on the belt securing his tunic. Clothes flew everywhere until soon, she felt the delicious sensation of flesh against flesh.

Sethe palmed her ass, his lips never leaving hers. Her breasts brushed against his chest, the exquisite sensation hardening her nipples. The dirt floor, the darkness, all of it faded away as she loved the man beneath her. Her hands flattened on his ribs, stroking, rubbing, down to his hips. She undulated on him, her slick folds caressing his cock with each stroke. His woodsy scent filled her nose, his taste on her lips.

He moaned as she pulled away, trailing her lips over his strong jaw. She nibbled on his neck, laving his Adam's apple with her tongue, then down to his collarbone. His flat pecs deserved attention, and she swirled her tongue over his nipples.

Sethe reached for her. He cupped her breasts in his hands, testing their weight. With his thumbs, he caressed her nipples, pinching them into tight little peaks before stroking them again.

Daphine suckled him, imagining it was his lips on her nipples. She delighted in the husky groans he made, the buck of his hips when she touched a sensitive spot. Her fingers danced over his flesh, following the arrow of hair past his navel, then lower, until she wrapped her fingers around his cock. Sethe's low groan only spurred her own desire.

She stroked him, base to tip, her lips descending ever lower. Moisture filled her pussy, her labia slick and plump with desire. Every inch of her body tingled, like what she felt at holy mass, only more urgent and more real. Her breath hissed from between clenched teeth when he reached for her, pulling her leg back toward his shoulder. He moved then, and settled his lips against her pussy.

Daphine moaned. His tongue speared into her, the action leaving no doubt as to his desires. Wrapping her lips around his cock, she drew it deep into her mouth. She laved it with her tongue, drawing tiny sounds of pleasure from her prince. The sensitive underside she sucked, until he thrust beneath her, and then she swallowed him, drawing her lips down his length until they were flush with his body. She hummed her pleasure.

She ate him, each slide of her lips over his cock making her think of him thrusting his rod into her slick channel. Beneath her, Sethe drew her clit into his mouth, sucking on it until she whimpered against him. Pleasure pounded through her veins. She bucked her hips, wanting to come.

Two fingers found their way inside her, and she worked herself on the thick digits. Sethe spread his legs, and she cupped his balls, stroking the tender skin behind. Everything he did to her, she wanted to do to him, until they both went up in flames. Her body clenched, pulsed. And then she came, shudders racing through her. Pleasure so intense she thought she might black out roared though her. She grazed his cock with her teeth, and Sethe stiffened beneath her. Cupping his balls, she felt them draw closer to his body.

"Oh Goddess," he moaned an instant before his cock pulsed in her mouth. Warm streams of come coated the back of her throat, and she swallowed greedily, each drop a sacrament. She licked him clean, then slid down his body. Her cunt still ached for him.

When she looked in Sethe's eyes what she saw nearly took her breath away. Love, pure love shone from his gaze. Almost reverently he cupped her breasts.

"I want you inside me," Daphine said.

Sethe's cock hardened. Reaching between her legs, she stroked him to readiness, his hands never leaving her breasts. He looked beautiful, sweat dampening the hair along his forehead, his body flushed with pleasure. Slowly, she lowered herself on him. Her head fell back with ecstasy. Her soft moans filled the air.

Sethe grabbed her hips. He thrust, slowly at first, then building up momentum, until Daphine's breasts bounced and her tiny cries came in time with the thrusts. "Yes. Yes. Oh Goddess, yes," she whimpered.

Her pussy tightened around him, and then ripples of pleasure rolled through her body. Sitting atop him, she spasmed, her channel milking his cock. Sethe stiffened. His guttural cries echoed in her ears, and his warm seed filled her. Daphine leaned forward and collapsed against his chest.

Sethe's arms wrapped around her and held her close. Her panting breaths slowed.

The door creaked open.

Daphine looked toward it, suddenly afraid of being found out. Sethe's arms tightened.

A man wearing the royal colors peeked inside. "My Lord," he said. "My apologies. I was just checking to be sure you hadn't come to any harm." An embarrassed flush crept over his cheeks.

"As you can see, I'm just fine. If you will wait outside."

Sethe gestured to the door, his other hand never leaving Daphine.

"Yes, My Lord. Of course, My Lord." He started to step away from the door. "And shall I announce to your parents that you have found your consort?"

Daphine's amused chuckle followed the man out the door. She cupped Sethe's face in her hand. "I don't know," she said. "Shall he?" She kissed him then, leaving no doubt as to the answer.

Also by Mary Winter

&

Ghost Redeemed
Ghost Touch
Once Upon a Prince (*anthology*)
Pleasure Quest (*anthology*)
Prodigal Son
Snowbound
Water Lust

About the Author

&

Mary Winter began writing when she was 16, using it as an excuse to skip gym class. She currently lives in Iowa with her pets and dreams of writing full-time. Her advice to anyone is: "Persistence pays off. Don't ever give up on your dreams!"

Mary welcomes comments from readers. You can find her website and email address on her author bio page at www.ellorascave.com.

SUMMER LOVIN'

Shelley Munro

Chapter One

ಐ

"Sophie Walker? Is that you?"

The dark-haired hunk grinned before grabbing me in a bear hug, right in the middle of the Burleigh Bowls Club.

Who was this Cutey Pie? My mind screamed questions even as I cozied up and savored the experience. I mean, what was not to enjoy? He possessed lots of muscles and was downright hunky with his tanned face and sexy grin. Pity we were in the middle of the Bowls Club. My heart kick-started into a racy beat, while I inhaled deeply to counteract the effect. He smelled wonderful — of ginger and exotic spices, all wrapped up with the tang of the sea.

Tall, dark and cute grasped my upper arms and pulled away before dropping a chaste kiss on my cheek.

Aw, call that a kiss, my inner siren taunted. Rev it up and lay one on me. For once I didn't care if I ended up being the floorshow. Like a kid in a candy store, I wanted to touch and taste. I wanted it all.

"Sophie, what are you doing here on the Gold Coast?"

I stared and still came up blank. The petite redhead who stood at his side didn't look too happy. If I was in her shoes I'd have felt exactly the same way. Possessive. Heck, in her place I would have bared my teeth and warned me off.

"I used to go out with Sophie's daughter," Cutey Pie said.

Redhead's frown smoothed out like magic.

I groaned inwardly. Well, that sure put me in my place. Cutey's name popped into my mind. Isaac Shepherd. I'd liked him back when Susan was going out with him. Since my daughter was notorious for being late, I'd spent a lot of time chatting with Isaac. We had a lot in common. It had taken me a long time to forgive Susan for letting him get away.

"Susan is married now," I said.

Isaac's brown eyes glowed, making me intensely aware of my body and the way my clothes fit. The word desperate came to mind. I hadn't kissed a man for a long time let alone got down and dirty. My hormones were protesting the lack of action. For a moment there, they'd thought they'd got lucky. Disappointment was a bitch.

"What are you doing here?" he asked, his husky voice strumming across my senses in a very delicious way.

"I've come over on a RSA trip, with a group of golfers. Ostensibly to keep an eye on my father, but he doesn't really need it."

"What's the RSA?" Redhead asked in her Aussie twang.

"Returned Services Association," Isaac answered.

"Hey, Sophie!" It was my Uncle James, my father's partner in crime. "There's a dance on here tonight. Fred and I are gonna grab us a granny!"

I did a mental eye roll. "You can't say that." After all, I wasn't exactly a spring chicken. My fortieth birthday was practically staring me in the eye, so I felt I should offer up a defense for the dozens of more mature women in the club. "It's not P.C."

"Aw, Sophie. Don't start," my father said. "Look at those women over there. If it walks like a duck…"

Scowling, I glanced in the direction Pop indicated. Three elderly women were giggling like young girls. I shrugged. I didn't intend to act the stern chaperon. Pop and Uncle James could get up to all the shenanigans they wanted.

"We must meet for a drink," Isaac said, sending a wave of flattered satisfaction through me. Bigheaded of me I know, but the redhead's scowls made me want to cheer. Score one for the visiting team.

"Why don't you come back for the dance?" Uncle James said.

One look at Redhead popped my bubble of optimism. Isaac wouldn't be here tonight.

Isaac glanced at Redhead too. "Maybe." His voice was noncommittal. "We have to go." His brown eyes caught my gaze, and for a long moment, we stared at each other. "It's been great seeing you, Sophie."

And damned if he didn't grab me and kiss me right on the lips. It was brief. Intense. And left my knees knocking. I stared after him in bemusement, my trembling fingers rising up to touch tingling lips.

A soft whistle from Pop jerked me from daydream land. "You've made a conquest there, Sophie."

"I'm old enough to be his mother," I protested, and inside, I railed at the fact. Sometimes, life plain sucked.

Uncle James looked me up and down. "You don't look your age. You don't look old enough to be that boy's mother. You're fit, you don't look like one of those god-awful beanpole models, and you have your own teeth. Always check the teeth," my uncle ended sagely.

"I'm not a damned horse!"

"No, you're a woman, Sophie," Pop said. "That's all any of us simple men want. A luscious handful of woman to cuddle up to at night."

He winked at Uncle James, and they both discreetly checked out the three giggling women over in the corner.

"Ooh, not while I'm looking," I said in a firm tone, although secretly, I was flattered, my confidence boosted. A bit of life in the old broad yet, I thought. I licked my lips and imagined I could taste Isaac. Damn, I didn't think I'd shower for a week.

* * * * *

I'll admit I wasn't looking forward to the dance. Another night of loneliness, but at least I'd be able to go shopping tomorrow while the others played golf.

We walked into the Bowls Club with the other twenty-two members of our group. The wave of conversation hit first, followed closely by the ka-chink of the slot machines and the faint clink of glasses. My nose picked out the scents—smoke, perfume, the old-fashioned aftershave favored by the men in our group and the enticing aromas of steaks and seafood wafting from the dining area.

"We're off to mingle. Don't wait up for us," Uncle James said with a wink at Pop, and before I could offer a protest they blended into the crowd. Great. I'd have dinner and head back to the accommodation. Maybe catch a movie.

"Sophie."

I turned on hearing the husky voice, and just like that the range of possibilities for the way I could spend my evening widened. As long as Redhead wasn't hovering in the wings. I peered behind Isaac but couldn't see a bodyguard. "You came," I said, a dopey grin forming. "What about—"

Isaac took my arm and led me in the direction of the bar. "We had a disagreement."

I wanted to ask questions, but his tone and set face discouraged my nosiness. "Too bad," I lied. "Can I buy you a drink?" I drank in his appearance, committing the vision of masculinity to my memory, so I could pull it out later and gloat that a young man had taken the time to socialize with me, an almost forty-year-old. He wore black trousers and a light blue, short-sleeved shirt. Nothing fancy, but then a man with his looks would display well in a ratty towel. Or nothing at all, I thought, mentally undressing him. Oops. My thoughts screeched to an appalled halt. A bit early in the evening for that sort of naughtiness. I hadn't even had a glass of wine yet.

In the next room, a band started up with a soft ballad.

Isaac took my hand. "Let's dance first."

Agreement froze halfway up my throat. I think I managed a creditable nod. All I could think was that I'd feel that hard wall of muscle pressing against my breasts again. Inwardly I trembled, worried at the direction my thoughts were taking. This could only lead to heartache. *Mine.* I hadn't felt this strongly about a man since my husband. Richard had been with the army and had died in a training accident when Susan was three. There had been a few men in the interim, but mostly I'd concentrated on raising my daughter. Now she'd married, there was a huge hole in my life.

At the edge of the dance floor, Isaac took me in his arms. Our gazes connected, making me swallow with sudden nerves. My nipples were tight buds, the friction of my flesh against lacy bra cups leading to a ricochet effect throughout my sensitized body. A wave of heat swept to my cheeks.

Isaac grinned, and it contained a quizzical quality. "Don't you want to dance with me?"

"Yes," I whispered, suddenly feeling as though I was saying yes to more than I was prepared for.

"Good." And he pressed me closer, stepping smoothly into a gap on the dance floor.

Our steps were perfectly matched. Isaac was only six inches taller than me so our dance didn't have the awkwardness that used to characterize my dances with Richard. I sighed inwardly, overdosing on his spicy scent. Being this close to Isaac was heaven and hell combined. The man was only a little older than Susan. I should have kept a decorous six inches between our bodies and chatted lightly about Susan and her husband and all the other things we used to discuss when Susan was running late. Instead, my breasts were flattened against his chest. Our legs brushed with each lazy step, and if I wasn't mistaken, he was *very* pleased to see me. It wasn't such a huge leap to horizontal thoughts. I drew in a soft, shuddery breath, namely to get oxygen to my brain and clear my thinking. Mistake big time. All I got was a lungful of Isaac's seductive scent.

Time to admit the truth.

I was aroused, dammit! And I wanted to jump this man so badly my stomach quivered and my sex ached. It had all happened quickly. So quickly, I was shocked because I didn't act this way when I was at home in Auckland.

The music slowed and stopped.

"Would you like to go somewhere else?" Isaac asked in a soft voice.

I studied his strong masculine features, but couldn't get a fix on how he wanted me to reply. So selfishly, I went with what I wanted. "Sure." Although my voice was noncommittal, my heart did an excited flip-flop. It felt like I was stepping into the unknown. In truth I was—I had no idea how Isaac felt or what he wanted from me. For all I knew, he could be dancing with me on a dare. The thought sobered me for five seconds, then the unconscious shifting of my feet sent a wave of sensation arrowing outward from my achy clit. Oh, man. I was in big trouble here.

Outside, the air was cooler. A soft breeze tugged at my curls, caressed my bare shoulders and sent my skirt swirling around my legs.

Isaac took my hand in his again. "Would you like to walk on the beach?"

Frankly, I didn't care what we did. I was too busy trying to put a brake on my unruly hormones. I prayed I'd get through the evening without embarrassing myself.

"Sure." A woman of many words.

"There's a bar at the far end of the beach. It's quieter than the Bowls Club. We can talk."

Momentary glitch. Isaac wanted to talk. Shit. Hell. Damn. My wayward hormones didn't think much of that idea, but I nodded. "Sounds great." My hormones would just have to get with the program.

"What are you doing with yourself now Susan is married?" Isaac asked.

"I haven't had a chance to make any plans," I said, trying to ignore the heat crawling from his hand up my arm. "She's only been married a month. I've been busy helping organize this trip for the RSA. I thought I might get an office job once things settle down. I'll probably need to retrain, but I'm willing to do that. I'm a quick learner."

"Good for you." Approval colored his words, and I felt as though I'd received an encouraging pat on the head. I basked in the support.

We paused at the traffic lights for the signal to cross, then headed for the beach. Hand in hand, we wandered down the Esplanade, the surge and retreat of the waves a romantic backdrop.

"Are you okay walking in those shoes?"

"Sure." I swear I have a bigger vocab than that, but my hormones were doing a real number on my vocal cords. Obviously, my blood was being rerouted to more important areas. Speech wasn't important when it came to sex. I cleared my throat, determined to show to better advantage. "What made you decide to move to Australia?"

Isaac seemed to hesitate. "I wanted a change. The bar I mentioned is at the end of this block. We can get something to eat there too."

Hmmm, nifty change of subject. I wondered at the story behind his move from New Zealand. "I am a little hungry."

"We can fix that." His gaze caught mine again and lingered.

Suddenly, everything was hot and heavy again—my body hungry for sexual release. He was going to fix that? Or give me food?

My mind worked busily as we neared the restaurant/bar. One glass of wine, I decided. I couldn't risk a drop more. For goodness sake, Isaac had gone out with my daughter. I shouldn't be having licentious thoughts about this...this boy.

"Sophie?" Isaac stopped walking outside a pavement café. All the outside tables were full. Laughter and good-natured chatter filled the air. "Sophie." He seemed uncertain, as if he was asking a question. Isaac frowned, hesitated, then drew me into his arms and kissed me.

Shock held me still. This kiss wasn't chaste. It wasn't hurried. This was the kiss that a man gave his lover. Instinct replaced surprise. My hands crept around his neck as I gave myself up to the pleasure of being kissed like a woman. His lips nibbled at mine, then his tongue traced along the seam of my mouth in a silent order for me to open for him. No problem there. My mouth opened, and his tongue slid inside. God, I couldn't believe it. A sigh of delight whispered from me at the surge and retreat of his tongue. He tasted, gently biting. Tormenting.

To my dismay, he pulled away. I wanted to grab his face and force his lips back to mine. Not finished. More! Please—heck, I was ready to beg if it would get me more of the same.

"I wanted to do that at the Bowls Club." He stroked a finger across my cheek and tucked a wayward curl behind my ear. "You haven't slapped my face, so I'm guessing you're okay with me kissing you."

A definite question. Okay. Moving right along here. "We could do it again," I said, a hopeful note clearly discernable.

His masculine chuckle held amusement, but his chocolate brown eyes caressed me as if he too, wanted more kissing. "Not inside the restaurant. My staff will take notes and give me a hard time tomorrow."

"Is this your restaurant?" I studied the bustling business with increased interest.

"Yeah." Isaac sounded uncharacteristically diffident.

"Looks busy."

His smile held pure sunshine as he opened the door for me. "I'm sure they'll be able to fit us in somewhere."

A few minutes later, we were seated at a corner table, the staff fussing over us. I intercepted a few curious looks and discomfiture bit me in the bum. I knew Isaac had been a few years older than Susan, but that still made him much younger than me. I fidgeted with my wineglass, my stomach jumping with nerves. Did I look desperate? Needy? Had Isaac kissed me out of pity? I glanced around the crowded room, searching out possible dates for Isaac. Good-looking and a successful businessman, he could have any of these women. Another thought crashed into front running. I'd turned into a cradle snatcher.

"Don't." Isaac stilled my hand by covering it with his own. "You're here with me because I asked you."

Slowly, I raised my head to meet his intense gaze. There was definite heat in his eyes. Did that mean what I thought, or was I reading more into the situation than warranted?

"There might be an age difference, but I don't care. We have a lot in common." He threaded his fingers through mine. "I kissed you because I'm attracted to you. There's no one else I'd rather spend my evening with."

"But—"

"But nothing."

"Okay," I said finally. "It will be lovely having dinner together."

The hand holding mine tightened. "Just so there's no mistake," he said, his voice gritty and low. "We're not going to stop at dinner. After we're finished here, I'm taking you to my apartment, and if I have my way, you're staying the night."

Chapter Two

ဢ

A tight sensation in the middle of my chest reminded me it was time to breathe. I sucked in a wildly excited breath, my heart racing with the strength of my emotion. I wanted to tell him we could go straight away. Why did we need dinner when we could have dessert? Cripes, I didn't want him to change his mind. Thinking too much was bad for the health!

"Think of it as foreplay," he said, almost as if he'd read my thoughts.

"Um…okay."

"Sophie, you don't have to."

"Oh, I *want* to." A blush swept through me on hearing the vehement tone.

Desire flared in his eyes, and instantly my mouth was dry, my body on fire.

Isaac cleared his throat. "How about if I order our meals?"

I nodded. Anything to get this show on the road.

"You still like pasta and seafood?"

I nodded again, making him laugh.

"A woman of few words." Isaac released my hand and stood. "Won't be long. I'll have the waiter get you a drink. White wine?"

"Please." I watched him stride through the restaurant. The view was stunning, a tight butt that made me conscious of mine. Frantically I tried to remember what underwear I'd donned after my shower. My forehead crinkled as I concentrated. Cripes, I couldn't remember. And on second thought, I didn't want to remember. Most of my panties were the plain cotton variety, and since my pregnancy, my stomach didn't suck in like a well-behaved stomach should. Eek! I inhaled rapidly to dispel my lightheaded panic. *What was I thinking?*

"Don't." A masculine hand settled on my shoulder. He planted a kiss on my upturned lips, and to give the man credit, he didn't even check to see who was looking before he did it. Isaac settled in the seat opposite me. "Don't you dare think like that."

"Like what?" I said, pretending innocence.

"If you're having second thoughts because you think it's too soon, that's okay. We can talk it through. If you're stressing because of the age difference that's another story." Isaac's face was deadly serious as he leaned over the table and caressed my cheek. He traced a blunt-tipped finger across my lips, and I fought the need to open my mouth and take his finger inside. My stomach fluttered while he seduced me with plain speaking.

"You have a gorgeous smile, beautiful blue eyes that remind me of the ocean on a clear day. Your hair is soft and shiny and reminds me of honey and sunshine. Your shape is plain sexy with gorgeous curves that make me want to touch. You're beautiful, Sophie. I'm not sure how old you are, but you don't look old enough to have a daughter of Susan's age."

"Thanks," I whispered, the lump of emotion in my throat threatening to choke me. The glow of honesty in his eyes made me feel beautiful.

"But that's not the main attraction, Sophie."

It wasn't? I felt my eyes widen in questioning mode. "Well, you can't be desperate," I blurted.

A bark of laughter escaped him. "I'm not. Work keeps me busy, but I have plenty of time to play. *If I want.*"

Oh, boy. The wicked glint in his eyes, echoed in his grin, told me he was ready to play now. My body tightened all over, even the stubborn stomach.

"It's your personality. You're a good person, Sophie, and I find that very seductive. Very sexy."

I resisted the need to fan myself. Yep, I was his for the taking.

A young girl arrived bearing a bottle of white wine. She showed the label to Isaac, and at his nod, deftly opened the bottle.

"Go ahead and pour, Gina," Isaac said.

When the waitress left, Isaac picked up my hand. A neat habit. I liked it because it made me feel special, as if I was important to him. For an instant, I pondered my underwear again before shoving the topic aside. I'd insist on the lights being off, and first thing tomorrow, I was off to the shops to replenish my smalls with lace and bras that screamed sex siren.

"How long are you over for?" he asked.

"Fifteen nights."

"Have you made any plans? Anything special you want to do while you're here?"

"Not really. I planned on a little shopping, some swimming, ogling lifeguards and general relaxation."

Isaac grinned. "There will be no ogling of lifeguards while I'm looking."

I lifted my hand in a cheeky salute. "Yes, sir!"

We chatted easily over our wine and our dinner, when it arrived—beautiful succulent seafood and a crisp Greek salad. Neither of us wanted dessert so we drank strong black coffee and nibbled on after-dinner mints.

Leaning back in my chair, I sighed in appreciation. I hadn't enjoyed myself so much for ages. Being with Isaac was like spending time with a close friend.

"Are you ready to go?"

Immediately, the sense of relaxation fell away. The silent message in him made my body spiral tight with need.

"Yes."

"You haven't changed your mind?"

"No." Not on your life. I was going to have mind-blowing sex. What was not to like?

Isaac had a quick word with his staff before leading me through the kitchen and out the back. I swear the kitchen staff stared holes through my back. Bet they were in the know about my underwear.

Isaac lived in a beachside apartment—a modern high-rise building with sweeping views of the coastline and easy access to the beach. I stepped out onto the balcony while Isaac poured us drinks. Lights twinkled all the way along the beach like a garland of stars. The muted pounding of the waves and soft music Isaac had put on created a seductive atmosphere, one that made me tingle with awareness.

"It's a lovely view," I called. "I could quite easily sit here for the rest of the week."

"You haven't seen the view from my bedroom."

"Oh." Oh, indeed. Wicked man. "And what's so special about your bedroom?" I asked when Isaac walked out carrying two balloon glasses of brandy.

He smirked. "First off, I'm there," he said with no regard to modesty. "There's a great view from the floor-to-ceiling windows. You can lie in bed and watch the scenery."

"Can the scenery see you?"

His eyes twinkled when he sank into a chair. "Only if they're flying by in a helicopter." He took a sip of his brandy and studied me over the top of his glass. "Don't you have a streak of exhibitionism?"

My brows rose. "Sex in a public place? Maybe when I was younger."

Isaac stilled me with a scowl. "You're not old, Sophie. Come here." He patted his knee, and the simmering lust inside me kicked up a notch. Things were about to heat up.

I set my brandy on the table. My heart pumped in rapid, unsteady beats as I closed the distance between us and sat on his lap. His arms came around me, and he pressed a moist kiss on my neck. The touch seared straight to my toes, sending a hello-get-ready signal to my pussy. My body moistened for him and I knew that nothing, absolutely nothing, was going to stop me having my wicked way with this man tonight.

He slipped his hand under my pink-and-white-striped shirt and splayed it across my tummy. In my shock, I forgot to suck in. Too late now, so I shoved the small vanity away as a lost cause. He'd felt one of my worst features and hadn't run for the hills. Of course, there was always the slight chance he might not like my butt. I don't think much of my rear end…

The warm hand on my tummy moved upward to shape a breast. Spikes of pleasure darted from wherever he touched. Oh, yeah. I was definitely in a bad way.

"Can I take your shirt off?"

"Of course," I blurted. Burning-hot color immediately collected in my face. I fidgeted on his lap, then suddenly became aware of his cock digging insistently into my ass cheek. I wriggled seductively, wringing a heartfelt groan from Isaac.

"Be still, woman."

Grinning, I kissed him full on the lips with tongue action and some nibbling. I brought out my whole repertoire. When I pulled away, we were both breathing heavily. I kissed the tip of his nose.

"You are one delectable distraction, Sophie Walker." The hand beneath my shirt slipped into a bra cup. Masculine fingers smoothed across my breast and gently teased and squeezed my nipple until it stiffened. I arched in eager acceptance, giving him easier access.

"Feels good," I muttered, deciding to start as I meant to go on. My husband, bless him, had done everything in silence and in the dark of night. I was a more visual creature who really got off on touch, taste, sight. I wallowed in using all my senses. I mean sex should be a decadent, sensual experience. No, I wasn't going to act the coward and hide in the dark as I'd decided earlier.

Isaac stood with a suddenness that made me squeak. I clutched at his neck, fearful of ending on my ass. Murmuring reassurance, he lifted me easily, and since I was in no danger of falling, I relaxed to enjoy the experience. "My bedroom," he said. "You carry the drinks." He bent a fraction so I could pick up both brandy goblets.

A minute later, I placed the glasses on a bedside cabinet and then bounced lightly on the huge mattress when he set me down. He flicked on the light, illuminating the huge room with a warm glow.

"I get to unwrap you first," he said, waggling his dark brows in a mischievous manner.

No arguments from me. I was already at the point where my clothes were a hindrance. Even the mystery underwear became unimportant. I wanted skin on skin and nothing else would do. Seeing my acceptance, his hands went to the small pink buttons on my shirt. His big hands trembled when he attempted the buttons, and I stilled him with a smile.

"Let me get the buttons."

His laugh was self-conscious. "I'm not usually this clumsy."

Knowing him as I did, it was easy to believe, and the thought warmed me. I liked the fact that he wasn't taking me for granted, that there were a few nerves in him as well. "Kiss me," I suggested, busily undoing my buttons. "And maybe take off your shirt so I can ogle."

Isaac straightened and rapidly stripped off his shirt. I stilled in the process of unbuttoning mine. He was gorgeous—an almost hairless chest with golden skin and just the right amount of muscles.

"I have to bite," I said in a breathy voice.

Isaac chuckled, the sound bringing a flood of arousal to my pussy. I fidgeted, half embarrassed, half triumphant at my body's excitement.

"No biting before I see bare breasts." He bent to rake his tongue across the soft swell of my stomach. A moan escaped me accompanied by a tightening of my womb. Yep, revved and good to go. I practically ripped off my shirt and tossed it on the floor, popping the back enclosure of my bra for good measure. Seconds later, my plain white bra hit the ground.

"Let's get the rest of the undressing done and out of the way," Isaac suggested. "As much as I want to unwrap you, I'm a little anxious."

"You're hiding it well," I said in a dry tone, my gaze darting down to visually measure the bulge of his cock beneath the black trousers. Always interesting to see the size of the package. Things looked pretty promising.

"You think?"

The trace of nerves in him steadied me. "Race you," I suggested. "The winner gets to bite first."

We both burst into a flurry of movement. Clothes flew in all directions, mingling on the floor with scant regard to gender. Isaac won, which wasn't surprising. I wore a few more clothes than him, and I labored under a handicap. One look at his bare butt and my fingers stalled, refusing to work. My mouth watered. I must have made a sound because he turned. And dammit, the full-frontal view was just as spectacular.

"Stay right there," I said in a thick voice. "Don't move a muscle."

"But I won. I get to bite first."

"Rain check," I said. "I'm not going to bite." I flung my remaining clothes to the ground and sank on my knees in front of him. "But I'm gonna taste and do some heavy-duty licking." I put a tentative hand on his thigh and glanced up at him. His eyes were heavy-lidded with hunger, and a tinge of color highlighted his cheekbones. His breathing was deep and a trifle unsteady.

I traced my forefinger the length of his silken shaft. He swallowed audibly.

"I can't believe I'm nervous," he confessed.

"That makes two of us. Or at least I was nervous." I curled my hand around his cock and pumped slowly. "Now I'm just plain horny. Sit back and let me play."

A laugh escaped him, the tension leaving his muscular legs. His hands cupped my head and threaded through my short curls. I released his cock and licked my lips, a tiny sigh of pure appreciation emerging at the sight. Swollen and extended full length after a few short pumps of my hand, the head was a purplish red. Steadying myself, I leaned close and licked the tiny slit at the end, breathing in his spicy scent at the same time. Isaac groaned, and a bead of pre-cum appeared. I savored the salty taste when I licked it away.

"God, do that again," Isaac demanded, his hands tightening in my hair.

I loved that I could drive him crazy with just the touch of my tongue. I ran the tip of my tongue along a prominent vein. His hips jerked when my tongue neared his swollen crown. Impatient to taste him again and drive him crazy enough that he'd beg, I took him inside my mouth. Yeah, I know. When it comes to sex I have a nasty streak. I like to tease, but I figured he should know this up front. So to speak. And I knew he'd probably get his own back.

My eyes fluttered closed and I dived into a world of sensation. His salty tang exploded in my mouth as I teased another drop of semen from him. His breathing deepened, and I encouraged him to thrust by taking him deeper into my mouth. Some women didn't like sucking off a man, but I didn't belong to that club. I gloried in the power, and the fact they were usually willing to return the favor didn't hurt a bit. A woman after the main chance—that was me. And, a tiny voice in the back of my head whispered, if you keep your mouth and hands busy, you might quit worrying about how weird this was—giving head to your daughter's ex-boyfriend. I froze as horror crowded my brain.

"Don't stop, Sophie. For God's sake don't stop." Isaac urged me on with both voice and hands, and I zoned out the inner turmoil to concentrate on pleasure. I slid my lips up and down his shaft, in and out of my mouth. I even used my teeth—just a fraction, a tiny scrape across the crown. It made him shudder, so I repeated the move.

Without warning, he jerked from my mouth and touch. I was standing on my feet, with his tongue halfway down my throat before I had time to blink.

His heart thumped steadily against my breasts and his arms wrapped around me so tightly I wasn't going anywhere in a hurry.

Gradually, he eased back on the kiss. I swear my knees knocked in time with my heartbeat.

"You are a great kisser," I whispered, almost drowning in the heat I saw in his eyes. Fiery heat that threatened to burn me bone deep. Bring it on. The idea of going up in flames with this man didn't worry me anymore. I had the rest of the trip for regrets.

"I'm good at a lot of things." The wicked smile that accompanied his words sent lust zapping the length of my body.

"Show me." It was an order more than a suggestion, but his grin widened into downright toothy.

"My pleasure, Sophie. You have no idea how much I'm looking forward to this." He scooped me off my feet and placed me on the king-size bed. The cotton cover was cool beneath my bare butt. His brown eyes swept the length of my body, lingered at my breasts. Lust made me tense and impatient. I wanted him inside me, his cock stretching me, filling me. But he took his own sweet time.

"You have beautiful breasts." Under his dark gaze, my nipples pulled tighter than they'd been before.

Slyly, I parted my legs, giving him a flash of pussy. "The view is great down here too."

Isaac chuckled. "I've have never had so much fun with a woman. It's always been about immediate satisfaction before."

"Sex should be fun. Satisfactory fun," I added.

"Amen to that," he said. "I'm going to taste you first, then it's gonna be hard and fast. You up for that?"

For the first time in my life, I managed a one-brow arch. Hot damn, I thought. Independent brows. I'd always thought this was an urban myth put out by romance writers. I glanced at Isaac's cock, and it pulsed in reaction. Ooh, a night of many firsts. "You're up for it."

"And I can be up for it throughout the night," he said.

I caught the note of seriousness in his words. His subtle way of telling me that in the bedroom an age gap worked for the benefit of both parties.

I waggled my fingers, parting my legs even farther so he couldn't help but see the view. "Come get me."

Isaac traced around the rim of my belly button with his tongue. A quiver worked through my body. In truth, the engine didn't need much warming up. He worked down my body, taking small nibbles from my quivering flesh, licking and kissing until fire roared through my veins. And he hadn't even got to the good bit yet. As the thought formed, he blew softly against my swollen folds. My clit jumped even though the whisper of warm air had only glanced across it. I smiled at the sight of his dark hair against my pale skin. Then Isaac distracted me. He combed his fingers through my pubic hair and gently parted the delicate lips of my folds. I tensed in acute expectation. He blew again, and this time I realized he'd purposely missed the main attraction.

"Hey," I said, trying to redirect his mouth.

"Patience," he answered, his moist breath a balm to my heated flesh. Then, his tongue darted out. He delicately traced the length of my slit. I froze, my breasts tingling in the fallout of his touch. Man, he had a clever tongue. It darted into the mouth of my pussy, collecting up some of the cream produced by my eager body. Like a cat, he lapped at my swollen folds, his soft sighs of appreciation pulling me tight as a bowstring. I vibrated, my head thrashing from side to side on the pillow. And still, he only stroked my needy nub enough to keep me primed. Not a whisker of a touch more.

"Please." The word was hardly more than a fevered pant. If my arms had been a bit longer, I would have redirected his mouth, but no cigar. I was forced to await his pleasure. My hips moved restlessly. I tried to time my moves, but he soon got wise and used brute strength to hold me still.

"Bully," I muttered. My hands plucked at my breasts, pinching nipples that ached and throbbed for his hot mouth rather than my own touch.

His head rose, and he licked his lips with a smacking sound. "I love the way you taste. I could lap at your cunt all night."

Normally, I wasn't one for coarse language. But in this context, my lover talking to me, the gritty language pushed my need higher.

I licked dry lips. "Let me come first. Please. After that, we should have sex proper. I want to feel you inside me. Then," I said in a prim, school mistress-type tone, "you can lick my cunt all you want."

Isaac tipped back his head and howled with laughter. I tried to act the indignant schoolma'am at first, but the humor of the situation got to me.

"You're not meant to laugh," I chided once he'd stopped. "You're meant to take action."

"Action, huh?"

I strummed my fingers across one of his flat nipples until it stood to attention.

Isaac leaned over to open the top drawer of the bedside table. He pulled out a box of condoms and took one out before dropping the packet beside the bedside lamp.

"Raised dots for added stimulation," he said with a straight face.

"You put it on," I said. "And hurry." I stroked my breasts again and arched my body. The insistent and savage ache between my legs needed tending. Isaac ripped the foil packet open and rolled the condom on. I slipped my fingers between my legs and strummed across my achy clit. My soft groan drew Isaac's attention.

His dark brows rose. He snagged my wrist, making a tsking sound. Lifting my hand, he sucked my finger into his mouth and licked it clean. Desire curled through me. Isaac leaned over, kissing me hard and passionately until I forgot my impatience. Brandy and a hint of my juices danced across my taste buds.

His cock nudged my thigh before Isaac redirected it to the mouth of my pussy. It had been so long. Isaac captured my lips again and pushed insistently into my womb. The sense of fullness was incredible as he buried himself to the hilt, but then he started thrusting.

Slow.

Deep.

Oh, boy. Deep was the best. And the way his thick cock stretched me, filling me so sweetly. I shivered and held on tight. Isaac stroked in and out, telling me I was beautiful, that he loved to fuck me. I gloried in his words, his touch. An orgasm shimmered just beyond my grasp. I moved with him, canting my hips high. Panting, my body tense, hungry for release. Isaac increased the pace, his balls slapping me with each plunge.

My eyes slid shut to savor and enjoy the intense pleasure, the strength of him as his thrusts grew more frenzied, working me, driving us both higher and closer to release. His head lowered and his tongue delved into my mouth, demanding. Plundering. I rocked against his body, his cock massaging my sensitive nub. He swept me under into a private place where sensation ruled and there were only the two of us. No past. No present. No rules about age. Just two lovers giving and receiving pleasure.

I sighed into his mouth at the beauty of it. Isaac hammered into me. We both breathed hard, straining for release. With each thrust, he pushed me higher. The insistent tingle each time he brushed my clit built. He pumped into me again, our lips grinding together. My hands smoothed over his back to cup his butt. I squeezed just as intense pleasure burst, washing over me in a fiery blaze.

"Isaac," I gasped, riding the wave for all it was worth. That seemed to be the signal he was waiting for. His strokes became frenzied, then he stilled, and deep inside I felt the pulsing of his cock as semen erupted from his body. He shuddered and squeezed his eyes shut in an expression that was almost pain. God, I loved that I could make him feel this way.

For long, silent moments, we cuddled, our sweaty bodies sticking together in a most uncomfortable manner. I didn't care. I hadn't felt this close to anyone for a long time, and I didn't want to move.

Chapter Three

℘

"You're squashing me," I protested, a full five minutes later. It wasn't that I wanted to move, but more I had to breathe. Isaac rolled off me, his sexy mouth curled up in a smirk. He dealt with the condom and then preceded to touch me, stroking his fingers through my slippery folds until the tingle I'd thought had finished, started up again. This time, he was more adventurous. His fingers smoothed my juices all the way up to my anus. An impudent finger pushed inside my puckered rosette and waggled.

"Ooh." Richard had never done that before. I decided I quite liked the stretching, invasive sensation.

"Has anyone had your ass before?"

"No," I said with caution.

"Not even toys inserted?"

"No." Then, with a random rush of words. "Did you sleep with Susan?" I don't know where the words came from—no, a lie. I knew all right. That old green-eyed monster called jealousy had me in a tight grip. A choke hold. The idea of Susan doing these things with Isaac was enough to make me uneasy. Me doing them, on the other hand, was quite all right.

Isaac removed his finger from my ass and sat up abruptly. "Curious or jealous?"

"A bit of both," I said, once again with caution.

His face was impassive. "Want to know details?"

"God, no!"

"I never slept with Susan." The quiet intensity in him told me he spoke the truth. "After I met you, I didn't want to."

"Oh." I swallowed, feeling none the wiser and more confused. What did he mean? After he met me? It didn't make sense. I was Susan's mother. Suddenly, I didn't want to talk. "Can we make love again?"

"Don't you have any more questions?"

"No." It was a lie. I had heaps of questions, but decided to bide my time. Some of the answers would come out in conversation. And besides, I'd been married and had a child. I was hardly in the position to act the jealous lover regarding things that had happened in the past.

Isaac reached for a condom and rolled it on.

"Wow," I said, impressed. "When did that happen?" The that in question was a very impressive erection. Thick. Long. I shivered at the idea of being impaled again.

Isaac grinned down at me. "You turn me on." Instead of coming to me, he lay down in the middle of the bed and tucked his hands behind his head. "Have at me," he said, his saucy grin all the dare I needed.

I clambered over his reclining body until my knees were either side of his thighs. My busy hands stroked his cock and fondled his balls. They were hard and drawn up tight. I licked my lips and looked up at the tiny sound he made. In that moment I decided to really put the past behind me. I'd wring every bit of enjoyment out of the next two weeks. Not every forty-year-old got to have hot sex with a babe like Isaac. I should make the most of it.

He reached out to stroke his fingers across one breast. "You're beautiful."

"Thanks." When he looked at me through his sleepy brown eyes, I felt beautiful. I bent my head and licked across his belly. The taut skin quivered beneath my ministrations. I worked my way down his groin, his straining cock rubbing against my cheek. I blew lightly across his balls. His hips bucked. Then, suddenly impatient, I moved. I raised my hips and impaled myself on his erection by tiny increments, enjoying the potent

male heat as he stretched me. When I was finally fully seated, we both sighed.

I flexed my sheath, squeezing my inner muscles around his cock. It felt damned good so I did it again. My pulse jumped, and Isaac's hips jerked. I lifted, slowly riding him, tilting my hips and experimenting with rhythm. My release was sudden and took me by surprise, roaring through me like a train passing straight through the station. I stilled. Isaac patted my thigh and flipped me over so my body was beneath his larger frame. Then, he thrust, entering me in quick choppy strokes, taking him to his release.

He rolled me back over, and I nestled against his sweaty chest, replete and sleepy.

"Go to sleep, sweetheart. I'll wake you later."

I was vaguely aware of him flipping off the light, plunging the room into darkness.

I woke to find him kissing me intimately, his head between my legs, his tongue stroking across my clit. He lifted me up to his mouth, lapping. Sucking. Nibbling. The man was *so* talented. I lay back and enjoyed the waves of pleasure building to a peak. This time was slower but no less intense as he dipped and delved and finger-fucked me into release.

"Incredible," I murmured, my voice thick with sleep.

"You're awake."

"Barely."

"Never mind." His laugh was dark and wicked. "I'm quite happy to do all the work." That said, he flipped me over onto my stomach. I heard the crinkle of a condom wrapper, then he returned and covered me from behind. His cock slid home, and he teased me into another awesome orgasm that left me limp as a spaghetti noodle and very satisfied.

I'd thought the next morning might be uncomfortable. It wasn't. Isaac shook me awake, had another condom on and was inside me before I could pry my eyes open. My muscles protested the vigorous awakening and my womb was a little tender, but a few kisses and seductive pulls on my nipples, a little stimulation of my clitoris, and I was his for the taking.

Later, after a shower, we sat out on the balcony, enjoying the midmorning sun. I'd borrowed one of Isaac's shirts while Isaac wore a pair of shorts and nothing else. We lingered over coffee, scrambled eggs and toast, and shared the paper. The best way to spend a lazy Sunday morning.

"Move in with me," Isaac said without warning. "I need to check in at work every morning, but we can spend the afternoons and most nights together before you have to go home. What do you say?"

My head shot up, his question distracting from the feature story about a drugs case being tried in Indonesia. "Yes." Joy burst through me. Easy decision. Why wouldn't I want to spend the rest of my holiday getting laid and having fun with Isaac?

"Great." Isaac reached across the balcony table to take my hand, his broad smile holding something that looked like relief. "Want to come to the restaurant with me this morning, then we can drive into the Hinterland or down the coast to Byron Bay?"

"I'm in your hands." I squeezed the hand that held mine and waggled my brows in a flirtatious manner. "Nowhere else I'd rather be."

"Saucy minx." Isaac checked his watch and stood.

My gaze wandered his chest, halting on a faint red mark on a pectoral muscle. My mark, I thought with a trace of smugness.

My man.

A breath stalled halfway up my throat, and the blockage caused an ache in my chest. I wondered where the possessiveness had come from. We'd slept together, and he'd asked me to stay with him until it was time to go home. I tried to dismiss our relationship as a holiday romance, but my heart told me it was more. I wanted it to be more. I scanned his gorgeous visage while he collected up the dirty dishes. How could I feel so strongly about Isaac when we'd only spent one night together? I glanced down at my bunched hands, my heart knocking against my ribs. It was a wonder Isaac didn't hear the racket. I thought about Isaac and puzzled about my feelings before I finally admitted the truth. To myself at any rate.

I'd started falling for Isaac when he'd been going out with Susan. That's why I'd been so angry and snappy with my daughter after they'd broken off their relationship. It had been a combination of jealousy and irritation because Susan had Isaac, and I hadn't.

Falling in love implied the possibility of a future. That couldn't happen. For a start, we lived in different countries. Isaac had his restaurant here on the Gold Coast while I lived in Auckland, New Zealand. We had the Tasman Sea between us, which was about the best contraception a relationship could have.

"Hey, why the glum face?" Isaac dropped into the chair opposite me, concern in his brown eyes. "You're not regretting last night?"

"No way," I said with easy conviction. To my relief, the worry faded from his expression. "I was wondering what to tell Pop and Uncle James. I think I'll go with the truth."

"And what would that be?"

A grin bloomed. "That I'm moving in with you for some hot sex."

* * * * *

Isaac offered to drop me off on the way to his restaurant so I could pack my bag and talk to Pop and Uncle James, but in the end I grabbed a cab. I let myself into our holiday apartment and found Pop making a cup of tea.

"There you are," Pop said. "Have a good night?"

"Of course she had a good night," Uncle James said, popping from the bedroom like the proverbial jack-in-the-box. "She's only just arrived home."

They both eyed me up and down as if looking for clues. Exhibit one. Luckily, the love bites on my breasts were covered under the layer of clothes I'd borrowed from Isaac.

"I…um…I'm going to move in with Isaac for the rest of our holiday," I blurted. I shifted from foot to foot, feeling unaccountably nervous about their reactions. A definite regression in age.

Pop grinned. "Good for you. About time you joined the land of the living."

"Looks like young Isaac has grabbed himself a granny," Uncle James said.

His words were a kick to my gut. They hurt, dammit.

"James," my father growled.

My feel-good mood seeped away. I sighed at the intrusion of reality. "It's all right. He's only saying what other people will be thinking."

"I'm teasing," Uncle James said, abashed. "Sorry, Sophie. Bad joke. I meant what I said last night. You don't look your age. Isaac is damned lucky to have you. Go and enjoy the rest of your holiday."

Pop grabbed me in a bear hug. "Have fun, Sophie," he murmured against my hair.

And just like that, happiness bubbled through me. For the first time in years, I was doing something for myself.

I tossed my clothes and toiletries into my bag and stayed to have a cup of tea with Pop and Uncle James before grabbing a cab to Isaac's restaurant.

Isaac was doing a stock take in the bar when I arrived. He scowled at the level of a vodka bottle while the rest of his staff set tables for the lunch rush and served the lingering breakfast crowd.

"Do you have a secret drinker working for you?" I asked as I dropped my suitcase on the floor beside the bar.

The scowl erased from his face like magic. "You're here." Two steps was all it took for him to close the distance between us. Heedless of the interested audience of employees, he kissed me as if he hadn't seen me for a month. It was a happy-you're-here kind of kiss underlined with the familiarity of lovers. I hung on greedily and milked the kiss for all I was worth, but at the back of my mind I realized Isaac had a few insecurities of his own. He hadn't been sure enough of me to confidently accept I'd return or keep my word. When we pulled apart, I heard, or didn't hear, the hush in the restaurant.

Then Isaac's barman spoke. "Just as well you're having the rest of the day off, boss. It's so hot in here, I don't think the air conditioner could keep up." The tall, skinny man fanned his face.

Isaac laughed easily, and I took his cue. "I missed Sophie. Besides, I'm the boss. I'm allowed. I'll have my cell phone with me if you need anything."

The barman nodded and moved along the bar to fill an order.

"Come on, Sophie." Isaac tucked his arm around my waist and picked up my case with his other hand. I smiled wryly. I wasn't going to get free anytime soon, given the grip he had on my arm, but I was fine with that. "I liked you better in the T-shirt and shorts I lent you to wear this morning," he said when we headed for his car. He swung my suitcase into the back.

"You wouldn't have been so impressed when the makeshift belt gave way and your shorts ended up around my knees. The cabbie thought it was hysterical."

Isaac smirked. "Bet you moved fast."

"You could say that."

"Would you like to go swimming?"

I nodded. Any time spent with Isaac was a jewel to treasure. "Sounds great. Are we stopping at your apartment first?"

"I thought we'd drop off your gear."

That day set the tone for the rest of my holiday. Lots of laughter, a little quiet time while Isaac took care of business and some great sex. Stupendous sex. Sex so hot that I thought I'd combust from the inside out. The only problem was that the day of departure was looming fast, and I didn't want to go home.

Chapter Four

ꕥ

I rode Isaac's cock slowly, stringing out release for both of us. A sense of bitter sweetness filled me. Isaac too, I think, since our lovemaking had held an edge of desperation during the past few days.

Increasing the pace, I angled my hips so each slide hit my sweet spot. I watched his face closely, taking in the stubble that lined his jaw. His eyes opened, and our gazes connected. I swear my heart went kaboom. With each passing day, with each touch and smile, the connection I felt for Isaac strengthened. I shied away from the obvious—that what I felt was love. It was too damned scary. And difficult.

"This is the best way to wake up in the morning," I said.

His grin lit up his face. He stroked his hands down my hips, then delved between my folds, dipping his fingers in my cream before skating them across my clitoris. His touch was enough to send my climax crashing over me. Isaac fastened his hands on my hips again and thrust upward, hard and with raw need etched on his face. A guttural sound came from deep in his chest. He thrust again with urgent hunger. Once. Twice, before he spilled his seed in hard, strong pulses. His release triggered another series of mini-explosions in my womb. God, I don't know how he managed to push me so high, but I wasn't about to complain.

I collapsed against his sweaty chest, and his arms wrapped around me. Gradually, our heartbeats slowed.

"Sophie, I want you to stay here in Australia with me."

I levered away from his chest to gauge his expression. Sincere. Maybe a hint of uncertainty. Not a suggestion of humor. He was deathly serious and nervous about my reaction.

"You want me to move in here?" I wanted to say yes so badly, but I also needed more reassurance. "With you? Permanently?"

"I love you, Sophie."

I closed my eyes, savoring the sound of the words. A lump of emotion clogged my throat, and I had to swallow before I could reply. I opened my eyes, a haze of tears shrouding my sight. "I love you too," I whispered. "I'll stay."

* * * * *

Pop and Uncle James didn't turn a hair at my announcement. They agreed to keep an eye on my house until Isaac and I had a chance to return to New Zealand to sort out loose ends.

I slotted into Isaac's life so easily it was as if my staying was serendipity. A part-time office job opened up at a real estate agent's office with the chance of increased hours in the future. I worked there during the morning and helped Isaac with his bookwork or did waitress duty if he needed a spare. I loved it. And I loved him.

I ran my hand across Isaac's naked back and pressed tiny kisses, tantalizingly brief across his collarbone. Isaac sucked on one breast, his cock pressing at the intimate juncture of my thighs. His hands dropped to cup my buttocks, lifting me in preparation for one seamless thrust.

"Hurry," I urged.

"We have plenty of time." The laughter in his words told me he intended to tease.

"Just wait until I'm in control," I said, wriggling, trying to force his cock into my pussy.

The doorbell rang. Not just one buzz, but long and loud as if the caller was leaning on it.

"Hold that thought." Isaac leapt off me and strode to the door.

"Ahem!" I said. "Clothes?"

He backtracked to grab a white towel and wrapped it around his hips before heading back to answer the door. Sexy. Very sexy.

Mine.

I leaned back against the pillows, my body aching for fulfillment. I pinched my nipple and thought about hurrying my release along. No. Not without Isaac. "Hurry."

"You got it," he called back, his voice throbbing with sensual promise.

The doorbell ceased. I heard a murmur of voices.

"You!"

Oh-oh, I knew that voice. I jackknifed to a sitting position and searched frantically for clothes. They were strewn across the floor where we'd tossed them in our hurry to undress last night. The clock ticked. I grabbed my robe from behind the door, put on an impassive face and sauntered out to face the music.

Attack. "Susan, what are you doing here?"

"Poppa and Uncle James wouldn't tell me anything." Susan actually pouted.

"I gave them a letter to give you." In that moment, I realized I'd spoiled my daughter, giving her everything within my power. "You could have rung. The phone number was there."

"I came to talk sense into you." She glared at Isaac. "Just as well I came."

"You remember Isaac." I indicated the silent man at my side. He looked disinterested, but now I knew him better I recognized his worry.

"I can't believe you're sleeping with Isaac." She looked him up and down in an insulting manner. "He's the same age as me!" Susan glared at his bare chest. "He could be your son."

"But he's not my son." I was amused rather than angry or abashed. And I wasn't about to let my daughter jerk my chain.

"Isaac is my lover." *Take that.* I'd let my daughter have her way, I'd spoiled her, but I really loved Isaac. I wasn't going to give him up because my daughter didn't approve. I glanced at Isaac before closing the distance between us. I curled my arm around his waist and leaned into him, inhaling his spicy scent. Silently, he hugged me, returning the encouragement. I felt the strength of his feeling even though no words passed between us. Emotion brought tears to the back of my eyes.

Susan stamped her right foot, propelling a bark of laughter from me. My grin and patent amusement prodded her temper. "You can't stay with him. Can't you see he's using you? You're easy sex for him!"

"That's enough," Isaac snapped.

I squeezed his forearm, and he subsided with a dark mutter. "Susan, contrary to your beliefs, I am an adult. I do know what I'm doing," a little devil made me add. "And believe me, there's nothing easy about the sex between Isaac and me."

Isaac laughed, and Susan whirled on him. "Is that why you broke up with me? Because of Mum. Was she the other woman you couldn't stop thinking about? The woman you loved?"

Isaac tensed. Both Susan and I observed him closely.

"I love Sophie. And I'm not about to apologize for it." But he wouldn't meet my eye. He looked discomforted.

He'd been attracted to me way back then? *Food for thought.*

"You want a mother," Susan scoffed.

I didn't believe that for a minute. The sex between us was too hot. Mutually fulfilling. We made love. We were equals. No way did I mother him.

The age difference meant nothing.

Time to take a stand. "Susan, I love Isaac. I intend to stay with him, and nothing you can say will change my mind. I've never been so happy."

"But what about grandchildren," Susan wailed. "You're so far away!"

I stared in shock. My daughter was a selfish brat. "Coolangatta is a three-hour flight from Auckland. I'm hardly on the other side of the world." Hmm. Children with Isaac. I hadn't thought about that…

Isaac brushed a kiss across my cheek, and I frowned at Susan. I wanted to drag Isaac off to bed and could hardly do it with Susan here.

"I'm pregnant," Susan blurted. She scowled at Isaac. "You'll be a grandfather, but you'll never be a father!"

"Congratulations, Susan." I kept my tone even, but my daughter was embarrassing me. She couldn't talk to Isaac like that. "Isaac and I will have children if and when we decide. Our relationship is none of your business. Get used to it. Is Michael here?"

Susan nodded miserably, her shoulders slumping. "He told me not to come."

"You should have listened to him," I said in a mild tone. "Where are you staying? Isaac and I will meet you for dinner tonight. We'll celebrate your good news." I glanced at Isaac and received a smile and a nod of acquiescence. My heart started to race when his gaze stroked across my lips.

"Paradise Grove," Susan said, this time a trifle diffidently.

"Good, we'll pick you up at six. See you and Michael later." I practically shoved my daughter out the door.

Isaac cupped my face between his hands. "I love you, Sophie. You'll marry me, won't you?" Emotion and love shaded his words.

"Have you really loved me all that time?"

"Yeah. I thought about asking you out, but the age difference was too great back then. Now it's not."

I kissed the tip of his nose, excitement and love dancing through me like a spring tonic. "You're a very wise man, Isaac Shepherd. Of course, I'll marry you."

"Aw, Sophie." Isaac rubbed his forehead against mine. "I love you." He paused, then grinned like a loon. "You do realize what your Uncle James is going to say, don't you?"

I thought and came up blank. "What?"

Isaac chuckled and hugged me tightly. "That I've grabbed myself a granny."

"Humph!" I mock-scowled, feeling so happy I wanted to cry. "That would make you a granddad."

Isaac's expression was priceless. I smirked. Nothing better than having the last word.

Also by Shelley Munro

∽

Curse of Brandon Lupinus

Men To Die For (*anthology*)

Scarlet Woman

Sex Idol

Summer in the City of Sails

Talking Dogs: Never Send a Dog To Do a Woman's Job

Talking Dogs: Romantic Interlude

Talking Dogs: Talking Dogs, Aliens, and Purple People Eaters

About the Author

Typical New Zealanders, Shelley and her husband left home for their big OE soon after they married (translation of New Zealand-speak: big overseas experience). A year-long adventure lengthened to six years of roaming the world. Enduring memories include being almost sat on by a mountain gorilla in Rwanda, lazing on white sandy beaches in India, whale watching in Alaska, searching for leprechauns in Ireland, and dealing with ghosts in an English pub.

While travel is still a big attraction, these days Shelley is most likely found in front of her computer following another love—that of writing stories of romance and adventure. Other interests include watching rugby and rugby league (strictly for research purposes *grin*), being walked by the dog, and curling up with a good book.

Shelley welcomes comments from readers. You can find her website and email address on her author bio page at www.ellorascave.com.

INTERPLANETARY SURVIVAL EPISODE #495

Tielle St. Clare

Chapter One

ဢ

"What are they?" Katya whispered, never taking her eyes off the four men standing opposite them. Their skin tones varied from light tan to a deep brown but each had a mane of golden hair forcibly constrained at the base of the neck. Fur jackets that matched their skin tones hung open at the front revealing broad, powerful chests and rippled abs.

But it was their tawny cat eyes that warned they weren't "pure-human".

"Riabhians. Human *descendents*," MarKaln, the team's information officer, said. "Some very strange genetic experiments were done in the years before Earth vaporized. And who knows what they've intermingled with in the two hundred years since."

"Giant cats," Katya joked. The smallest of them was a good seven feet, maybe more. Humans had grown taller through the centuries but had stalled at the mid-six foot range. She watched the way they stood—arrogant, aggressive and sensual—like they were assessing whether Katya's team was worthy of their notice. There was something definitely feline about them—not the tame versions she'd seen in twentieth-C vids, but wild ones like they kept in zoos. Brutal, dangerous and sexual.

Her mind drifted to the possibility of curling up with a kitty like one of them. They all appeared quite capable of keeping her warm and toasty. A shiver skated down her arms. She'd been cold for three of the four weeks they'd been in this competition. Once they were done, she was leaving this frozen planet and going someplace warm. And if they actually won, she would use her share of the prize money to buy a beach on some planet deemed too close to its sun. She pressed the collar of her "all-weather" suit shut. The revolutionary material was supposed to keep the wearer warm through the worst conditions. Obviously the makers had never been to this planet. Cold, wet and occupied by a notoriously unfriendly race.

Jessup, their team leader, pushed his shoulders back and scraped his hair away from his handsome face as he approached the Riabhians. The saunter he used as he walked forward was pure sexual animal and Katya knew it was designed for the lone vid-cam that tracked them. The other vids had moved on ahead, keeping up with the race leaders.

All four giants listened intently as Jessup spoke. He was in his "I'm just one of the guys" mode. It worked with most males. It seemed to have no impact on these guys. The one in the middle shook his head and then spoke. The negotiation was on. Jessup listened intently, then slowly nodded.

The vid-cam swirled around, getting a shot of Jessup's face. The red light above the lens clicked on indicating the camera was being taken live. What could Jessup say that would interest the race organizers enough to take their vid-cam live—pulling attention away from the leaders?

The Riabhians turned their catlike gazes to Katya.

Jessup spoke again. The four warriors listened and their eyes went from arrogant to appalled. Whatever Jessup had offered them wasn't what they'd expected. The lead Riabhian nodded but ignored Jessup's proffered hand. Jessup laughed like it was a friendly joke then turned to face his team, a confident smile on his lips.

Katya's heart pounded a little faster. They'd agreed to something. This might work. They were a day behind the leaders. If they could get passage through the Riabhach Forest, they could make up that time and more. They might *actually* win this thing.

In the four years she'd known Jessup, all he'd talked about was forming a killer team for the InterPlanetary Survival Race. Of the competition shows that had sprouted up on vid-nets everywhere in the past five years, this was the most brutal and prestigious. The challenges were hard and the rules few. They had to get from one end of the planet to the other using any means necessary.

Jessup glanced at the camera with a cocky smile and winked. Whatever he'd done, he thought they had a chance now.

When they'd started this game, she and Jessup had talked about a future together—sharing their half of the prize money—but now she didn't know. They'd drifted apart, which wasn't easy when there were only four of them traveling together. Jessup spent most of his time playing to the ever present vid-cams.

Jessup left the Riabhians but instead of returning to the team, he called Katya over.

The vid-cam floated behind him, the red light still glowing.

The center of her stomach began to burn as she crossed the small clearing. Conscious that their conversation was being recorded, she kept her voice casual.

"What's up?"

"They're willing to let us through their forest. Safe passage."

"Great."

"For a price."

"Can we afford it?" The organizers of the game gave them a set amount of credits to use during their travels. They were low on cash.

"They don't want credit. They want to barter."

"For what?" He didn't answer. The burning in her stomach turned into a slow, sickening roll. "Jess, what's the price?"

"You."

"What?!" She didn't attempt to keep her voice down.

"Their demand for safe passage is one night with you."

"You aren't serious." Even worse, he couldn't seriously be considering it. But when she looked at him, she saw he was. "You expect me to whore myself so we can walk through their forest."

"It's the only way we're going to catch up." Jessup's jaw tightened. "We're too far behind." *And it's your fault.* He didn't say the second part but she heard it just the same.

It *was* her fault they were behind. A violent bout of food poisoning last week had slowed them for a day allowing the other teams to outstrip them. Jessup would have left her behind but all team members had to cross the finish line for a win.

"We need this."

She opened her mouth protest but the glint in his eye stopped her. His gaze made a quick flick toward the vid-cam that hovered nearby. He was playing to camera. Jessup was setting her up to take the blame if they lost.

"How many do I have to fuck?"

A twitch in his cheek was the only sign she'd shocked him. "Uh, just one."

"Okay."

"You'll do it?"

Katya almost smiled. Jessup wasn't going to like seeing his jaw falling open and his eyes bulging broadcast on vid-screens across the tech-world.

"Sure." She leaned forward, placing her lips close to Jessup's ear, too close for the vid-cam to monitor. "But I want half your share of the prize money."

"Do you know what that'll leave me?" he hissed.

"Twice what you make in a season, and you'll have won." There were dozens of endorsements, interviews and appearance opportunities that would make up for what she was taking. And he'd get the fame he desired.

"Fine."

She smiled sweetly at Jessup and fluttered her eyelashes. "Then I'll go meet my date for the evening." With a flip of her hips, she spun around and approached the four huge men. The closer she got, the more intimidating they were, looking less human with each step.

Two of them grinned with undisguised interest as they scanned her body. One looked at the ground like he was embarrassed. But the middle one boldly undressed her with his eyes. Not the largest of the group, he was the most frightening. She glanced down, surreptitiously checking out his body, and imagined she saw claws poking out the ends of his fingers.

Please let it be one of the others.

With a confidence she didn't feel, she slipped her hands into her back pockets and lifted her chin in defiance. "So, who's my lord and master for the night?"

Bach stared down at the little bit of a woman before him. The saucy tilt of her head was in complete contradiction to the fear in her eyes.

"That would be me."

She took a long, deep breath as if bracing herself for the trial ahead and nodded. "Then let's get this going."

Bach raised his eyes to Jezran, his second-in-command, and nodded.

"Come this way." He opened his hand indicating the small thatched hut that stood on the forest's edge. The points of his claws were visible at the tips of his fingers. He left them out, warning what she would face if she followed through with this. The woman stared at his hand then pushed her shoulders back and walked forward, her eyes trained on the cabin. Never looking back for a moment of support or sympathy from her team.

The vid-cam sped toward them, as if intending to follow — but Bach held up his hand, sending it away. He wasn't part of their game. Obediently, the vid-cam stayed back but the red light didn't go off.

"If you don't want her, I do," Jezran said softly.

Bach's upper lip pulled back into an instinctive snarl. "If anyone's having her, it's me."

"You don't sound sure."

"I think she's playing me." He cocked his head back toward the remainder of the woman's team. "Watch those three. Any man who'd sell his woman can't be trusted."

Bach stepped into the hut, his eyes immediately adjusting to the darker surroundings thanks to the cat genes integrated into his system. His ancestors had arrived on this planet as little more than animals with human forms — barbaric, more wild than tame. And they'd taken control of the land. After four generations of intermingling with humans Bach believed they had the right mix of instinct and thought. Neither gave him any clue why she had agreed.

Did she want to win this game so badly? Greed was a powerful motivator. Though his people avoided interaction with pure-humans he knew what success would mean to her. Money, notoriety.

A sorrow that a woman as appealing as she was would sell her body for a prize.

As she looked around the bare room, Bach took the opportunity to inspect her. Her hair was cut short like the women of his world, her body tight and sleek. She moved with the sensual sway of a pretty cat. The sight of her long legs and the sweet curve of her ass sent signals to his cock that his brain tried to ignore. He wasn't an animal that would mount any attractive woman. First he would discover why she was here.

After her exploration of the one-room cabin, she faced him. He approached slowly, drawing closer than a human would find comfortable. She leaned away then stopped as if realizing what she was doing. The human had strength. Courage. Intriguing qualities in a female.

She led with her chin, simultaneously pressing her chest forward. The slight mounds of her breasts were a delicious distraction but Bach trusted his other senses. The delicate fragrance of woman was smothered by the scent of annoyance and fear.

"You don't want to be here."

She raised her chin even higher, baring her neck, daring him to claim her, fuck her. He would have—if he thought she had any idea what her pose was inviting.

"Don't worry." Her voice held the arrogance of a woman used to being in charge. The sound sent him into a brief foray of fantasy. Her, commanding him in the bedchamber, ordering him to pleasure her repeatedly with his tongue. The sensors along the sides of his tongue tingled with anticipation. He crushed the feeling. She took a deep breath and said, "Jessup made the bargain and I'll fulfill it."

He swallowed to crush the laughter. This little bit was bold and blunt—but she wasn't as tough as she appeared. If he truly took her up on the offer, she'd run screaming from the hut, back to the comforting arms of her leader. They were lovers. Bach was almost sure of it. So why had the man offered up his woman?

"Are you sure, sweet one?" Her heart started to pound. The pulse vibrated into his body and settled into his shaft. He leaned down, brushing his lips against her ear. "I can smell the fear in you.'" As he said the words, he detected a new scent—arousal, muffled by fear, but growing. Bach stepped away. "What's your name?"

"Katya."

He smiled.

"Katya. It means 'bright kitten' in our world."

Her shoulders softened a little but with a quick pull she straightened again. "That's sweet. Now, shall we get on with this?"

He didn't move. With an annoyed sigh, she ripped open the snaps that bound her jacket closed. The thin undershirt she wore hid none of her form. Her breasts were on the small side but the nipples pressed tight against the stretchy material were clearly defined and ready for his mouth. Unfortunately, he knew it was from cold not desire. She grabbed the lower end of the undershirt, clearly preparing to strip before him.

"Do you not care about my name?"

She stopped. "Uh, sure. What's your name?"

"Bach."

"Nice to meet you, Bach, now can we do this?"

He laughed. He couldn't help it. She was determined to go through with it and equally determined not to enjoy it.

"Why? You don't want to do this and you clearly expect little pleasure from it."

"Don't worry. I can fake it."

He grinned. "So can I."

When he made no move toward her, Katya sighed. What was the problem? This had been his idea in the first place. She just wanted to get it over with. No, she *wanted* to be miles from here but she wasn't backing down. Not now. That damned vid-cam was no doubt circling the hut to see if she reneged on the deal. There was no away she was leaving.

If only Bach would cooperate. What was wrong with him? The inhabitants of this world were supposed to be highly sexed.

At least her would-be lover wasn't hideous. He was attractive enough though his eyes were disconcerting. Amber eyes with the oval iris of a cat—but what worried her more was the fear that he saw too much with those eyes. The long blond hair intrigued her. Her fingers twitched with the anticipation of feeling it on her skin.

Well-developed canines appeared when he grinned at her. He was definitely part animal. Unfortunately, he didn't seem to have any intention of attacking her. He didn't even appear interested.

"You aren't going to do it, are you?" she accused. "You never planned to fuck me."

"No."

"Why not?" *What's wrong with me?* She didn't dare ask the question. It sounded a little too desperate. It wasn't like she *wanted* to have sex with him but why didn't he want to have sex with her?

"A test. We had no intention of letting anyone through our woods."

"So, you demanded the price of fucking someone—"

"Yes, and each of the previous teams who requested passage decided the price was too high. Yet your leader offered you up as prize. I'm curious why you agreed."

"I have my reasons. But now, you have to let us through. We agreed to your price." He grimaced and it was her turn to laugh. "Shot with your own stunner."

"Exactly."

A ripple of relief ran through her. She wouldn't have to fuck him.

The bargain. Damn. If she didn't have sex with him, he could back out of it. She had to do it. There was no way she was walking out of the cabin not having paid the price for passage. Jessup would know. And the vid-cam would be tracking her every move.

But this big cat didn't seem inclined to follow through.

She was going to have to seduce him.

Chapter Two

‬

It's time to end this game. Bach started toward the door. Katya jumped in front of him.

"No. Neither of us is leaving this room until sunrise."

For the second time this day, Bach was startled by this woman. She wasn't going to let him leave without a fight. He could understand. If he left now they'd think she wasn't willing. Her team captain looked like the type to remind her later that she'd failed the team.

"Fine. We'll stay until morning." He nodded to the high mattress. "The bed is yours. I'll—"

"No. The bargain was for sex. I fuck you—we get safe passage. We're doing this."

She couldn't be serious. One look at the determined glint in her eyes and the sharp jut of her chin warned him she was. What did she expect to do? Seduce him?

"Even if I don't want it?" His cock leapt inside his furs to voice its dissenting vote.

She tilted her head to the side and smiled. "Are you sure you don't?" In a move that was as old as time, she trailed her finger across his lips and down his chest, sliding his furs open, and tracing the tip of her finger around his nipple. The rebellious point popped forward. Her eyes held his as she leaned forward and opened her mouth against his chest, laving her hot tongue across the tiny peak.

Bach snapped his teeth together, fighting the animal instincts that clawed at him. With his lips squeezed shut to suppress a groan, he inhaled through his nose. The fragrance of fear had faded—arousal hummed beneath her natural scent. She liked what she was doing to him. Enjoyed the act of seducing him. She scraped her teeth across his skin, nipping at the last moment with a bit more force. He grunted and the perfume from her cunt filled the cabin. The cat senses bred into his people captured it, savored it.

She lifted her head and smiled at him—deliberately seductive with a hint of laughter. She knew she was getting to him.

He had to stop her. He wasn't fucking an unwilling woman. "Don't worry, I'll still—"

She grabbed the lower edge of her top and ripped it off. Before it hit the ground, she reached for the buckle of her pants, tore it open and dragged the material down.

Mere seconds and she was naked. The animal inside him roared. Instincts his ancestors cherished demanded he take what she offered. His cock pressed against the shaved fur that covered his legs. The sleek muscles of her legs told him she'd enjoy a hard ride. The peaked nipples on her smallish breasts stretched toward him, silently begging for his mouth.

Katya stepped away, blatantly baring her body to the man before her. She arched her back to make her breasts look bigger. Bach's eyes followed the movement, going lower to her hips, legs, pussy. She peeked at his groin. There was a definite bulge. He was interested. All she had to do was get him to fuck her. Once—that's all she needed.

She considered reclining on the bed, touching herself while he watched but that left him too much opportunity for escape. Instead, she walked forward, slipping her hands beneath his heavy fur coat. Hot hard flesh slid beneath her palms as she eased the coat off his shoulders, sending it to the floor. Closer, she had to be closer. She pressed against him, brushing her breasts against his bared chest. Wicked heat shot from her nipples to her pussy, melting her insides and the moan that escaped her lips wasn't contrived.

Letting her body lead, she raised up on her tiptoes, startled by the growing pressure between her legs, the dampness in her cunt.

A sharp spike spun through her pussy as she circled her clit against him. It felt so good she had to do it again. Dazed and seriously confused, she moved into him, needing the delicious pressure building in her pussy.

"Kitten, you're going to get caught." The warning in his voice was clear but the need inside her demanded release. She rubbed against him as she scraped her teeth across his strong jaw.

Bach growled and spun her around. The sudden withdrawal jolted her from the sensual daze. Cool air brushed her nipples but Bach's heat covered her back. He held her there, his hands at her waist, his covered erection pressing against her ass. He was big. Her pussy twitched at the possibility of taking the thick rod she felt into her passage.

If only he would cooperate. A reminder of why she was doing this tried to seep into her brain but she pushed it aside.

Feeling like a sex show performer, she leaned forward, placing her hands on the mattress and pumping her backside against him.

Bach looked down at the perfectly formed ass massaging his erection. She canted her hips, sliding his cock between her ass cheeks. He couldn't stop the groan as he settled into that warm delta.

He grabbed her hips and thrust against her ass, warning her what would follow if she didn't draw back. She didn't retreat. She spread her legs and rocked into him. Wet heat from her pussy seeped through his furs.

His control wavered.

Take her. It's what she wants.

He could smell her arousal now. Her fear had faded and all that remained was hot, sexual female. Her cunt was wet and open. For him.

"Fuck me." Another slow pulse of her hips followed the breathless plea.

Animal instincts battled human restraint. The creature his ancestors had been rose to the surface and it wanted, *needed*, the sweet cunt that begged for his penetration. His mind faded to black as he ripped open the flap of his trousers. His cock leapt forward, settling between the sweet warmth of her thighs.

Soft, wicked heat enveloped him. Bach clenched his teeth, trying to convince himself that she didn't want this…but her wet pussy contradicted him.

Hunger drove him, pushing him on until he placed his cock against her opening. Hot viscous liquid slipped from her cunt, coating the end of his shaft, easing his way as he pressed inside her. A thin voice of restraint held him back.

"Damn it, fuck me!"

The human half of him fought, knowing she didn't truly desire this. But the animal ruled, needing the sweet fire of her cunt.

He thrust forward, driving deep and hard, listening to the ancient creature inside him. Her cry shattered the silence even as hot, wet flesh drew him deeper. The harsh rise and fall of her shoulders and the renewed tension in her hands told him she was preparing herself to take his brutal fucking. All for that damned bargain.

He stared at the tight connection of their bodies. What was he thinking? He wasn't an animal. He started to withdraw.

"No!"

The firm muscles of her ass tightened as she rocked against him. He froze, holding himself still as she moved on him, fucking herself on his shaft. The slow, steady pulses were like a band around his cock, tightening, squeezing until he thought he would explode.

The sharp pumps continued, hard and shallow, mechanical.

Bach bared his teeth and snarled at the dying light in the room. The kitten thought she could make him come. Thought she would force him to climax inside her while taking no pleasure for herself. She just wanted him finished.

She should have thought of that before she dared me to fuck her.

Bach wrapped his arm around her waist and held his cock inside her.

Katya groaned and struggled against his grip, the delicate little pulses blinding him for a moment. He smacked his hand across her ass. She snapped her head back and glared at him. It was the first real emotion he'd seen from her. He tapped her butt again. Her pussy clenched around his shaft.

She likes to have her ass spanked.

"Just get on—"

He repeated the smart tap, a little harder. She groaned and this time when she rolled her hips into his, he knew it was desire not design that moved her body.

"You wanted this, you'll have it." He held her still and gave a shallow thrust inside. "My way."

She dropped her head forward, resting her forehead on her crossed wrists. "Yes. Do it." The martyred tone made Bach smile.

"Don't be too upset if you enjoy it some."

Bach withdrew slowly, letting every inch of his shaft caress her pussy as he retreated. The sleek line of her back called to him and Bach stroked his hands down the smooth length, letting one claw scrape across her skin, reminding her she wasn't dealing with a human she could control. Her body undulated, moving into his touch.

"That's it, kitten. Feel me." He pushed into her. "So sweet. I'll have all you." The clasp of her pussy eased, luring him deeper. He fucked her slowly, in and out, finding the perfect rhythm until they both wanted more.

"Bach." His name—breathless on her lips as she accepted him—released the animal inside him.

Basic energy surged through him, making him push deeper, harder. The sweet pussy around him opened to him, hot and commanding. No power could stop him. He needed to come inside this cunt, needed to feel her climax around him. Bach dropped his head back and roared at the ceiling. The claws curling from the tips of his fingers gripped her flesh. It felt so good, so hot.

He held her hips and rode her hard, driving every inch he had deep into her cunt. Her cries filled the cabin and Bach accepted them, taking them as his prize. He pounded into her, losing himself in the sweet grasp of her cunt, feeling her take him again and again.

"Aaah." She groaned and pulsed against him. He pushed into her and held himself there, giving her shallow thrusts, sensing the deep caress she needed. "Noooo. Too much." The whimper drew him back.

"Come for me, kitten."

Her groan was like a fist around his cock. He couldn't resist. He drew back and fucked her, hard and deep. The ripple of her climax and muffled cry sent him over the edge. He filled her again and let the power take him, flooding her cunt with his seed.

She collapsed onto the mattress but their bodies stayed locked together. Bach held his breath, listening to his heart pound, staring at the delicious form beneath him. He wanted more, wanted all of her.

His cock hardened inside her.

She gasped and moaned, moving against the rising pressure. Her pussy was still wet. She could take more. Take him again.

Animal instincts demanded he drive his teeth into her, marking her as his, claiming her. Mating her.

But he wasn't an animal led only by his urges and she wasn't a woman for his world. In the morning, she would leave.

She'd fulfilled the bargain. He could expect no more of her.

Take her, fuck her.

Fighting the rising desire, he withdrew and stepped back. She pushed up from the bed and faced him. Her cheeks were red from the exertion and her eyes glittered with a stunned kind of satisfaction.

His cock bobbed between them.

Her gaze fell to it and Bach waited. She'd fulfilled her part of the bargain. She could leave.

She lifted her eyes and a mixture of satisfaction and wicked intent stared at him. The pink tip of her tongue slipped out and traced the upper curve of her lip. Watching the blatant motion, he realized he hadn't tasted her, not the flesh between her thighs or her tempting full lips. It was a craving he couldn't ignore.

Katya's mind clouded as he leaned closer. This was probably a bad idea but with the traces of a killer orgasm singing through her veins she couldn't remember why. The ache in her pussy grew as his lips floated over hers. She groaned, imagining his mouth on her cunt—soft and delicate, deliberate.

He sampled her lips, light sweet kisses that teased and tempted her until she was chasing him, needing more. She lapped her tongue along the peak of his upper lip then snagged his lower lip between her teeth, gently biting down. When she released him, his eyes burned with the ancient passion of his ancestors. He dragged her body against his and angled his mouth over hers. *Now* he conquered, tasted, controlled, his tongue filling her mouth, calling her to accept his power.

His hands gripped her thighs and he lifted, pulling her up and spearing his cock into her cunt. Her startled gasp lasted only a second. She blinked and stared up at him.

The dare was visible in his eyes. Would she accept him again? His hard length filled her, reaching parts she hadn't known existed. The power to speak was gone. She wrapped her legs around his back showing him that she wanted him.

His hands held her ass, pumping her up and down his length. She tried to convince herself that she was doing this for the bargain but, oh, she wanted him. Wanted that delicious cock riding within her.

He slipped his hand between their bodies and rubbed his thumb across her clit, shooting Katya to a quick bright orgasm.

As she opened her eyes she realized he was still hard...and she was in for a long night.

Chapter Three

༄

Dawn crept above the horizon. Bach felt it in his veins, felt the power of the land as it awoke. His cock arose with the same energy. The warm sexual body beside his immediately consumed his attention. Katya. Goddess. Sexual. Sweet. Moving without thought, he rolled over, easing himself between her thighs, his cock finding the warmth of her cunt. He slipped into her as she came awake. Her green eyes fluttered open and she stared at him. He waited, knowing she could reject him, knowing she wouldn't. He pressed deeper, soft and slow, feeling her pussy ease for him. He kept his thrusts gentle. She had to be sore. He'd lost count of how many times she'd come, and he'd filled her with his seed at least four times.

"Once more," he said, needing the final pleasure.

Part of her mind whispered she'd fulfilled the bargain but she knew the truth. This was no fuck for safe passage. She wanted him. Needed him. Inside her.

"Yes," she said, curling her arms around his neck. They didn't speak. No teasing or whispers. Their moans and sighs speaking for them. His gaze held hers—the gold flecks in his cat eyes glowing as he pumped inside her, deep heavy thrusts.

Her chest tightened, making it difficult to breathe. Before last night, she hadn't understood that so much pleasure was possible. And now she would have it, one last time.

He dug his elbows into the mattress and held himself above her, his cock riding sweetly inside her. The angle pressed the tip of his shaft against the top of her cunt. Each push magnified the pressure, one sensation on the next, until she was clinging to him, begging him. She covered his chin and jaw with desperate kisses, whispered hunger.

"Please, let me come. I need to come." Her cries became desperate pleadings as he rocked deep. "Bach, I need you. Please."

"This cunt belongs to me," he growled. Vicious need filled her core, flowing into her sex. "Mine to fuck."

"Yes!" Even as she cried out, he moved, his hips pumping hard, filling her deep with each thrust.

"Take me," he commanded.

"Yes. Mine. Yours. Oh yes." She knew she was moaning random words. It didn't matter. The delicious pressure grew until she couldn't contain the sensation. She screamed, clutching him to her as he roared and his cum shot deep inside her body.

Bach dumped the wash water out the back door and watched Katya dress. Her movements were quick, efficient. The seductive woman from the night before was gone. Pushing her shoulders back, she walked to the door, not looking at him as she said, "Thanks."

Thanks? Bach shook his head, feeling ill-used by the wench. She'd fucked him, welcomed him into her body and walked away.

A nudge from his conscience reminded him that he'd arranged the bargain in the first place.

Now he had to ensure them safe passage. He could send Jezran along with them. Jez knew the woods better than anyone. Bach opened the door.

"Good morning." Jez greeted him but his eyes tracked Katya's ass as she walked away. Bach's teeth stretched downward and he knew he wasn't letting Jez guide them into the forest. He'd have Katya on her knees as soon as they'd disappeared around the first bend.

Bach followed Katya down the path, keeping a small distance, not wanting to add to her embarrassment of facing her companions. As she reached their camp, the two other men stood. The looks of concern irritated Bach. Where was their concern last night when their team leader was offering her as a passage price?

"Are you all right?" the shorter one asked. The huge man beside him nodded. The vid-cam swirled around them focusing on her face. Its red light glowed like a demon's eye.

"I'm fine."

"But we heard a cry—"

"I stubbed my toe."

Bach choked on his laugh. The garbled sound drew the others' attention. The short one pulled himself up to his non-impressive height and glared in Bach's direction.

"Don't, MarKaln. Jessup made the agreement." Katya patted the warrior's shoulder. MarKaln relaxed but didn't take his eyes off Bach.

"About time you're here." Jessup approached, his hair wet. And no doubt chilly. Jez would never direct these men to the hot springs.

As Jessup neared Katya, her body changed, going from calm to tense. Her chin jutted out, her breasts pressed forward. Jessup moved close, closer than most humans would like. Too close for Bach's pleasure.

"Are you all right?" Jessup's voice dropped to an intimate tone.

Katya raised her chin even higher and stared him in the eye—daring him to contradict her. "Why wouldn't I be?"

The concerned look on his face didn't match the anger in his eyes. "Did he hurt you?"

Her tinkling laughter sounded real as she shook her head. "Don't worry your little head about what happened inside that cabin."

She turned away, leaving Jessup alone. They all watched as she knelt down and checked the pouch of her backpack. Whatever was going on in her mind, she wasn't sharing.

Jez approached, giving Bach two water gourds which he draped over his neck and shoulders, forming a crisscross on his back. The sun was just breaking the horizon. The heat of the day — not that it differed much from the night — was on the rise and they needed to travel while it was light.

"We should go," Bach announced.

"You're not going with us," Jessup said stepping close to Katya. The move was intimate and protective and it was all Bach could do not to rip the human's arms off. A bright tingling crept up his neck and his canines lengthened at the sight of Jessup so near his woman. Before Bach could move, Katya stepped away, out of Jessup's protection. She wasn't letting him claim her. The animal inside him growled its gratitude. She would never belong to the human again.

"The bargain was safe passage through our forest. You'll need an escort to survive."

Jessup grimaced then nodded. "Fine. We're moving quickly so you'd better be able to maintain a steady pace."

Katya laughed and earned a glare from Jessup. She pulled her pack on. "Trust me. For him, stamina is *not* a problem."

After two hours of steady running, the forest had become a blur around her. After four, she focused solely on placing her feet in Bach's footsteps. Lack of sleep began to weigh on her. The patented material of her suit was designed to wick moisture away, keeping her cool but when they stopped she remembered how cold this planet was. She looked at Bach. He'd removed his fur coat and had wrapped it around his waist. The strong etched muscles of his back were marred by faint scratches on his skin. Katya knew she'd put them there and the sight was a constant reminder of the night.

He'd stuck to her side all day. Not intrusive or commanding. He'd talked when he had something to say — pointing out interesting sights in the forest — but otherwise kept quiet. When they'd stopped, he'd stepped close. Giving her the protection of his body, a sip of his water, offering her his coat. He hovered near as if ready to guard her from any danger.

She could have told him she didn't need pampering or protecting but for some reason the words wouldn't come. It was nice to have him beside her. Their conversations though limited were interesting and enlightening. He clearly loved the forest. His pride and loyalty to the land allowed him to creep into her heart a little. She'd always wanted a place that she could claim, one that called to her soul. Bach and his people had found it.

They pulled up to a stop and Katya gratefully sipped some of Bach's water. She had her own but his tasted fresher and cooler.

Jessup scanned the sky. "Where's the vid-cam?"

"Called back," MarKaln said. "Something about its batteries. It's supposed to catch up with us later."

"Fuck." Jessup glared at Bach as if it was his fault. "If we had any chance, they never would have pulled it away. After all we've done, we're still going to lose this damn thing."

Katya looked at Bach and rolled her eyes. He winked at her and took off, walking until the team had caught up with him and then moving into a slow jog, making sure Kat was behind him. They ran for two more hours. The sun was on the decline when Bach pulled to a sudden stop and slapped his hand out, catching Kat across the waist.

"What?"

"Don't cross that line," he said, indicating a thin line of rocks that intersected their trail.

"Why the fuck not?" Jessup demanded, stalking to the front of the line. "We're trying to win a race here."

Bach shrugged but wrapped his arm around Kat's waist, holding her to him. "Your choice." He paused just long enough for Jessup to consider the idea. "We'll just step over your body as we pass."

Jessup moved forward.

"It's his forest, Jessup," MarKaln called.

"He's just fucking with us," Jessup said. Hatred filled his eyes as he glared at Bach.

"Then go." Cold surrounded Bach's voice indicating he didn't care if Jessup lived or died.

"Don't," she said, adding her plea to MarKaln's. She didn't love Jessup anymore. Didn't even respect him as a leader but she wasn't ready for him to die. "Bach knows these woods. If he says stop, we stop."

Jessup looked down at her. The hatred turned into a snarl. "Fine. But if we lose you get nothing. Remember that."

Katya looked up at Bach, silently apologizing for Jessup. Bach just shook his head and she realized she didn't need to apologize. Nothing would ever change his opinion. Jessup had sold her and for that Bach would never forgive him. Pleasure swirled through her stomach. He would never sell her. He would never even consider it. If the offer had been made to him, the man would have been dead before the words left his mouth.

On impulse she stretched up and planted her mouth square on Bach's. She felt his shock as she grabbed him but seconds later he was fully involved, his mouth, his hands, caressing her, moving across her back, holding her against him. She lifted her head and couldn't conceal her smile. It made no sense but she felt good around him.

A breeze swept by them and Katya couldn't stop the shiver that zipped down her back.

"Come, you're cold." Bach moved to the side of the path and sat down on a large rock. He picked her up and settled her on his lap. Warmth immediately flowed into her skin. He untied his coat and draped it around her, creating a warm, dark tent.

"What the fuck are we supposed to do?" Jessup demanded, planting himself beside them. Bach didn't even acknowledge him. "If you won't let us move forward, what are we supposed to do? Watch you two fuck?"

Bach's jaw began to ache. Before this trip was over he was going to throttle this human. Until then, he would play with him as only a cat could.

"Wait."

"What the fuck for?" Jessup demanded.

Bach stared at the other two men on the team. They looked away as if ashamed of their leader. Bach dismissed them. They didn't support Jessup but neither had they protected Katya when he'd sold her. They would be punished by their own Gods.

But Jessup. He would be made to pay. Not only had he offered Katya, he'd once been her lover. For that, Bach would kill him.

"We wait for Bresnak."

"Who the fuck is Bresnak?" Jessup demanded.

Bach looked to Katya. "Why does he use passion as a curse?"

"He doesn't understand."

"What *the fuck* are you talking about?" Jessup demanded.

Katya laughed and Bach felt himself smiling along with her. Strange since meeting her, he'd smiled often.

She makes me smile.

He heard his father's voice whisper through his memory. Bach had asked his father how he'd known his mother was the right woman for him and he'd answered "she makes me smile". Bach turned to the woman lying in his arms. He could tell from the light in her eyes and the taut strength to her body that she wouldn't make life easy but it would be fun.

"Who is Bresnak?" Since the question came from Katya, Bach answered it.

"He's a...I'm not really sure what he is. Definitely not human, or not totally. Only a few of his kind exist." He shifted, pulling her closer, feeling her tight ass press against his growing erection. Her eyes twinkled as she felt the pressure. "They're vicious, strange and nomadic. Bresnak moves his camp when he chooses and wherever he marks his territory belongs to him."

"And you never know where that's going to be?" Her voice sounded hazy and slow.

Bach shook his head, tightening his arms.

"Aren't you guys supposed to be the tough ruthless killers?" Jessup demanded. "Just get rid of it."

"Why? He doesn't harm our land. Takes little for his needs. And his ancestors were here first. I see no point in denying him passage through our land."

Jessup didn't seem to have an answer for that. Pure-humans rarely did. Katya was silent and Bach realized she'd fallen asleep, her head against his chest, her body curled into his. His ass was going to freeze if he sat there much longer but there was no way he was moving her.

"Seek you access to the great and powerful Bresnak's lands?" The ringing voice yanked Katya from her sleep to see the nearly naked man before them. *Nearly* naked because he was wearing a leather shoulder covering and boots, but the rest was bare. Even in the dying light she could see the full erection between his thighs.

Bach lifted her off his lap, gently setting her on the ground before he stood. Her body was stiff as she stood and the sun was set. She had no idea how long she'd been asleep.

"We seek to cross Bresnak's lands, taking nothing, leaving nothing behind."

The man bowed sharply, wrapped his hand around his cock and spun away, disappearing into the trees. He must be freezing.

"Uhh." Katya held up a finger, trying to phrase her question.

"Bresnak demands that his servants be ready to fuck at any time," Bach answered before she spoke.

"And the women?"

"My women are wet and eager for me at all times." Katya turned to find the source of the voice and gasped. He sounded human but the creature that walked out of the trees was clearly not. It—he—was huge, a foot taller and wider than Bach. His skin was brown and scaly, mimicking the tree bark around them. His eyes were bright red—all three of them. The only part of his body that appeared smooth was the huge cock that swung between his legs. Like his servant, he was hard. A small crowd of naked people hovered behind him. Their greedy eyes skipped from person to person and Katya had the distinct impression they were deciding who to fuck first.

Bresnak approached and Katya struggled not to retreat. The predatory gleam in his eyes made her tremble.

"Who do you belong to?"

Her first reaction was "no one" but she realized that was a bad idea. Every independent impulse in her body rebelled but she pointed to Bach.

"Him."

Bresnak didn't look away.

"He fucks you and gives you pleasure?"

"Yes."

"He fucks you well and each night?"

"Yes." *Oh yes.*

"You bear his kits?"

The thought made her heart stutter. Kits? As in children? It was rare for women of her world to bear children. They had droids for that. But this creature would know nothing of this.

"Not yet, but soon."

Bresnak dragged his gaze down her body, his third eye focused solely on her sex.

"You are a prized mate," Bresnak announced. "Bach claimed you. He may keep you." Bresnak swung around and faced Bach. "If you do not honor her, I will take her, fuck her until she screams with pleasure and cannot remember your name."

Bach bowed his head, acknowledging Bresnak's command and hiding his own smile.

"Come. We will eat and you will pleasure your woman."

Bresnak and his minions turned and walked back into the dense trees.

"Stay close tonight," Bach whispered to Katya as they followed. "Things could get interesting."

Chapter Four

෨

They fought their way through ten feet of thick brush until they broke through and came to a clearing.

A fire burned brightly in the middle of a rock circle. Bresnak's people had cleared the snow away and placed therm-pads on the frozen ground, giving them ample sleeping space. Around the fire, women scooped a hot liquid into chalices. Bach removed one of his water gourds and handed it to MarKaln.

"The food should be fine but don't drink anything that's offered to you."

MarKaln raised his eyebrows but accepted the water.

At Bresnak's command, Bach led Katya forward, sitting across from Bresnak in the inner fire circle. Heat from the blaze warmed the air but Bach still guided Katya to sit between his thighs. It was a blatant sign of ownership and Bach wanted to be sure Bresnak saw it.

One of Bresnak's women approached, smiling as she offered them a chalice. Bach waved her away. MarKaln and Terance watched him and did the same. He'd enjoyed Bresnak's hospitality before but doubted Katya was ready for it.

After a short time, food was brought around and Katya ate the bits Bach picked out for her. Bresnak sat across the fire, his third eye locked on Katya. Women and men approached the strange creature, kneeling before him, stroking him. He accepted their caresses then sent them away.

Katya sank deeper into Bach's embrace. The therm-pad kept the snow from freezing their backsides but the air was still chilled. It was hard to believe Bresnak's people were naked. She looked around the fire circle. Bresnak's people cuddled in small groups, couples and threesomes — touching each other, kissing. No doubt keeping warm.

"I warned him."

Katya followed Bach's gaze and saw Jessup accept a cup from the man who'd greeted them on the trail. Jessup looked defiantly at Bach and took a long swallow.

"Is it poison?" Katya asked.

Jessup was smiling as he lowered the cup. "No, but he'll have an enlightening night." Another man joined Jessup and the first guard. Jessup smiled and kept drinking, talking with the two men who watched him with avid interest.

"Come, Bach, past time to be fucking," Bresnak called.

Bach swore under his breath.

"What?"

"He's waiting for us to start."

"Start what? Fucking? Here?" Bach nodded. "In front of everyone?"

"They won't watch long. As their guests, they want proof we have found pleasure." Bach tilted his head toward MarKaln and Terence. "Have you a place for them? It is not allowed for kinsmen to see their women engaged." Bach's people had no such rule but he didn't want Katya embarrassed. She would be uncomfortable with her teammates nearby and watching.

Bresnak nodded. The two women kneeling at his feet stood and led MarKaln and Terance out of the clearing. Two other women left their partners and moved to Bresnak's side.

Bach scanned the crowd. Jessup was gone as well. Good. Bach grabbed a blanket from a pile behind him and stretched out, pulling Katya down beside him. He tossed the blanket around them.

"Bach?" The disgruntled call came from across the fire.

He raised his head and smiled at Bresnak. "My woman is modest." He covered them with the blanket up to their heads.

"Don't worry," he whispered to Katya. "We don't have to do much. Just enough to give them some inspiration."

Her eyes twinkled in the pale light and Bach found himself smiling again in return. "Oh, I think we can inspire them."

He realized she rather liked the idea. His little kitten had as exhibitionist streak in her.

Katya glanced toward Bresnak. He nodded, giving her permission to begin.

She rolled on top of Bach, pouring herself over him until her knees straddled his hips. The hard bulge of his erection fit perfectly between her thighs and she was tempted to stay but she wanted more. She wanted Bach's eyes to glow with golden light and hear that delicious roar as he came.

The smooth skin of his chest was barely visible through the opening of his jacket. She pressed the fur aside, baring more skin, slipping beneath the blanket as she kissed her way down. His stomach tightened as she lapped at the hard muscles.

As she reached for his trouser flap, Bach lifted the blanket edge. "You don't have to do this," he whispered.

She looked up and her lips spread into a wide grin.

"I know."

He dropped the blanket and stared up at empty night sky. Devilish heat followed her mouth as she worked her way down his body. Her hot little tongue, tasting him like he was her favorite sweet, the delicate stroke of her fingers.

He fought the pleasure, knowing she would stop. When she realized she didn't need to follow through, she would stop.

She opened the flap of his furs and freed his shaft. Her breath warmed his skin an instant before her tongue fluttered against his cock. He held himself still, enduring, loving the long strokes, her lips, tongue and fingers worshiping his cock. The multiple caresses wove a fiery web around his shaft hardening it further.

She wrapped her hand around the base and licked her way up to the thick head. Bach held his breath, waiting, needing. Eternity passed before her mouth engulfed his cock, accepting more than half inside. He cried out, his hips punching up in a compulsive thrust. He needed more. Katya seemed to hear his silent pleas. She rose up and knelt, her ass a delicious shadow beneath the blanket as she bobbed up and down, her hands working along with her lips and, oh, Goddess, her tongue was pure earth-fire.

A low hum rushed from beneath the cover, a groan as if she enjoyed it as much as he. The delicate caress compounded the pressure in his tormented body and Bach released it, struggling to hold still and not drive himself to the back of her throat as his cum exploded into her mouth. She didn't pull away. Instead she licked and soothed him until his shaft began to wilt.

Bach turned his head and met Bresnak's fiery eyes. The creature nodded his approval.

Energy and need surged through her as she climbed up Bach's body. His amber gaze greeted her as she emerged from the blanket. It had been delicious having his cock inside her mouth, feeling him hard against her tongue. She licked her lips and felt his cock twitch against her leg. Her pussy fluttered in anticipation.

Low groans rang through the air and blended with slaps of flesh meeting flesh. Katya looked at Bresnak. Two of his three eyes were closed, the third was still locked on Katya. He knelt behind one of his women, his huge cock pounding hard into her pussy. The glorious pleasure on the woman's face made the ache between Katya's legs worse.

She needed to be fucked.

With a smile for Bach alone, she bent down and stroked her tongue across his nipple. His quiet gasp told her clearly he wasn't finished yet. She pushed up on her knees and reached for her trouser snaps. Bach's eyes tracked the motion of her hands even as he held the blanket over her.

"No one's watching," she whispered, though the possibility that someone might see was ever present in her mind.

"Vid-cam."

Her heart melted at his consideration. He had no reason to care. He lived in the forest and had little contact with the tech-world.

Under the blanket's cover, she wiggled and shimmied until her pants and underwear were gone. It felt deliciously wicked with both of them mostly dressed, only their groins bared and ready for each other. She knew from the previous night that Bach recovered quickly and wasn't surprised to feel his erection pressing against her thigh.

She curled her hand around his cock and petted it, loving the smooth, hard shaft, tracing her fingers along the thick vein. And while she stroked him, she sensed his cat eyes watching her. The pure fire that burned in them rushed moisture into her sex. She had barely been touched but she was eager to take him. His hands held her knees as she shifted, positioning his shaft to her opening.

Slowly she sank down, remembering how big he was—how tightly he fit inside her. Two inches slid into her but soreness from last night's fucking slowed her. Taking a deep breath, she drew back, riding those first few inches until her pussy begged for more. She pushed farther, sending him deeper. That's what she wanted, more. All of him.

"Open your top." The growled command broke her concentration and she sat up, settling him fully inside her pussy. Their groans joined the sexual sounds around them.

She smiled and took a few breaths, letting her body adjust to the fullness.

Bach licked his lips as she undid the snaps of her jacket. She started to slide it off her shoulders but he stopped her. "I'm not sharing."

Her nipples were clearly defined against the thin material of her undershirt. He closed his mouth over one peak, sending a renewed need into her pussy. She pulled back and yanked the bottom of her shirt up, baring her breasts. For once, she had no worries that she was too small. Bach's pleasure was reflected in his eyes and the wicked strokes of his tongue.

Katya moved with him, rocking in sync to his licks, riding her pussy along the hard shaft inside her. It didn't take much. Her body grabbed the sensations and shot her to a quick, hard climax. Bach lifted his head and smiled.

"Pure pleasure."

He latched on to her nipple and began to suck. Katya dropped her head back and moaned. It was too much. She wanted more. She wanted to fuck him. Drive him insane. Barely finding the strength to deny her body, she pushed on his shoulders. A disgruntled look crossed his face as he fell away.

"Kitten—"

"My turn," she said.

Chapter Five

ஐ

She leaned forward, holding herself over him as she began to ride him, sliding his cock in and out, hard fast pumps. "This is what you want, isn't it?" she whispered against his ear. She nipped his skin with her teeth, still fucking him. "To fuck me. Feel my cunt holding your cock."

Bach's neck arched up and his lips pulled back revealing long, sharp canines. The human was struggling for control.

His hands left her thighs. She looked down. Claws popped from his fingertips. He buried the sharp talons into the pad beneath his hips, tearing the thick material. He was fighting the beast inside him. Letting her fuck him as she wished. She knew he could have pulled her down, plunged his shaft into her but he was letting her lead.

Power and pleasure exploded inside her. She moved faster, taking him deeper, pulling back until he almost slipped from her but stopping, keeping him inside her where he belonged.

"You feel so good inside me." She covered his mouth with hers, driving her tongue between his lips. When she drew back he chased her but she shook her head. "So hot and hard. For me. All this for me." She bit his shoulder, pumping against him, faster and harder, each stroke pressing against her clit until she rode him for her own release. Hot spikes pierced her hips as Bach's hands gripped her, pulling her down to meet his upward thrusts. The hard fuck was just what she craved. She sat up, not caring who could see her. Throwing her head back, she cried out as the pleasure broke inside her. Bach's roar joined hers as his cum filled her again.

They settled on their sides, facing each other. Her body pulsated with the lingering embers of her climax, filling her with heat even as he warmed her from the outside. She lifted her head and smiled.

"I'm warm."

Bach's satisfied eyes turned to her. "What, kitten?"

"The only times I've been warm since I came to this planet have been when I'm next to you." He placed his hand on her back and drew her near. Katya draped her knee over Bach's hip, opening her pussy to his renewed erection. Bach raised his eyebrows in question. She wrapped her hand around his cock and snuggled closer, positioning him at her entrance. Answering her silent command, he pressed his palm against her ass and guided them together, his shaft easily sliding into her.

She groaned deliciously as their bodies reconnected. "Hmmm, now I feel warm inside too."

Light flared in Bach's eyes, rewarding her for letting him see her pleasure. They lay together, bound, and talking in low voices. Shouts of climax occasionally shattered the silence, reminding Katya that she was filled with Bach's cock.

She stroked her hand over his tightly bound hair. "Do you ever let your hair down?"

He rocked his shaft inside her, the subtle movement blurring her senses.

"When a boy reaches manhood, he lets his hair grow and binds it back until he is mated. From that day forward, only his woman will see his hair down."

"Why?"

The edge of his mouth kicked up. "Tradition. Warriors wore their hair back during battle and only when they felt safe did they release it."

She reached up and slid a single finger into his hair. "So no woman has ever seen your hair?"

He shook his head. The air around them seemed charged as he pulled her hand down to his mouth. He gently kissed the tip of her finger, nipping the end with his teeth. Lengthened canines glittered in the dark light and Katya remembered how easily he could harm her. His strength could overwhelm her but even at that first meeting, she hadn't feared him.

Their eyes stayed locked together as he moved inside her, slow, shallow pulses. She'd never be able to come from this but it was lovely to feel him move inside her.

He tensed and placed his hand on her lower back, pushing her hard against him.

"Close your eyes. Don't move." The click-whir of the vid-cam reached her seconds before the red scanning pattern began tracking the fire circle. She closed her eyes and dropped her head on Bach's chest. Sleeping wasn't interesting. The vid-cam's controllers would move on. With her eyes shut, she sensed the scanner moving over them. It paused and she knew it was recording the fact that she was sleeping in Bach's arms. But after a dozen heartbeats, it retreated.

Bach watched the camera spin and twirl, searching for the other team members, no doubt hoping for something more interesting. It flew in the direction of MarKaln and Terance but returned moments later. The bright lens spun back and forth and then headed into the woods, tracking Jessup's path. Bach smiled. It would be interesting to see what the camera found in the forest.

Katya returned from the river, shivering but clean and dry. The other women ran naked through the cold back to the warmth of Bresnak's camp. They laughed as they huddled around the fire. The camp was empty except for the women. Katya slipped around the crowd and crawled back under the blanket still warm from Bach's body.

Seconds later, he walked out of a small hut. MarKaln and Terance followed. The three came to her side—Bach kneeling behind her and sharing his warmth. Heat returned as he surrounded her.

"Where's Jessup?" MarKaln asked after they'd finished breakfast. As the question left his mouth, the team leader appeared, walking from the trees. He glanced at Katya and she could swear he was blushing.

The two guards appeared from the same stand of trees.

"Just what was in that drink?" she asked Bach.

"Something that reduces your inhibitions and heightens senses."

"So they…?" The question about what they'd been doing evaporated as the vid-cam flew out behind the guards.

Jessup nodded toward the trail, ignoring the two men behind him. "I'm assuming we can leave now."

Bach stood and approached Bresnak. The two males talked and shared a laugh before Bach returned. "Bresnak's cleared our path."

They trudged through the brush back onto the trail. Again Bach took the lead. He didn't take off in a run today but a fast walk, keeping Katya beside him.

Though physically tired, energy pumped through her well-loved body. They talked as they walked. She learned more about Bach's people and the ancestors who'd come two hundred Earth years ago, and why he stayed in such a frozen world.

Two hours after they started, the trees came to an abrupt stop. The sharp spires of a city were visible in the distance, no more than a few miles away.

"That's Piscian," Back said, nodding to the bright city before them.

They'd made it through.

Bach turned to Katya. It was clear he wasn't going any farther.

"Uh—" She looked up at him and the words wouldn't come. They'd only known each other for two days so why did it feel like she was leaving part of herself behind?

"Good luck, kitten." Bach raised her hand to his mouth and kissed the back of her fingers. That delicate caress wasn't enough. She needed one more taste. She pressed up on her tiptoes. He met her kiss with a groan and their tongues tangled together, sharing flavors, remembering tastes. Breathless, she stepped back.

"You're disgusting," Jessup sniped. Bach lifted his head, his lips pulling back in an instinctive threat. But Jessup wasn't looking at him. He was staring at Katya. She lifted her chin in defiance of Jessup's disdain. "He's not even human."

Bach laughed and placed another kiss on Katya's fingers, drawing Jessup's attention. "You hypocrite." He pierced Jessup with his stare. "You expected her to fuck me but you're pissed that she might have enjoyed it."

"Let's go." Jessup grabbed Katya's arm and yanked her toward the city. Katya ripped her arm out of his grip. She looked up into Bach's eyes and saw the true power that he held. Jessup saw it too and began to back away.

"I'm fine," she said, drawing Bach's focus. "Forget about him."

"If he puts his hand on you again, I'm going to rip his arm off and beat him to death with it."

Despite the fury that buzzed through Bach's system, she smiled. He was still defending her.

"Thank you," she said, placing a light kiss on his cheek. "For everything."

"Good-bye, kitten."

"Good-bye, Bach."

Trailing behind her team, she took off in a run, her feet crunching on the hard snow. They reached the crest of the first hill. Jessup raised his fist in triumph. The finish line was in sight and the glowing green ball indicated no one else had crossed.

"We can do it. Let's move."

Katya looked back. The entrance to the forest was empty. Bach was gone. Her heart hung heavy as she turned and followed her team down the hill.

Katya fidgeted as the camera turned toward Terence. It scanned him, then MarKaln, her and on to Jessup. She had to admit, he looked stunning, rough and ready, a little dangerous. Many women would dream of him tonight.

Katya would be dreaming of another — Bach.

The hostess smiled at the camera and began. "So, of course, we're going to start with the unprecedented move that put this team in the lead, ultimately winning the game for them." Jessup resting his arm on his knee, his face proud and confident. "To get passage through the Riabhach Forest, Katya, the female on this team, agreed to a night of sex with one of the dangerous creatures who control that part the planet." The hostess spun around and faced them. The woman's eyes twinkled with anticipation. "That was an amazing sacrifice you made for your team. Katya, tell us how you survived."

Katya shared a woman-to-woman smile. "Trust me, it was no sacrifice."

The first interview over, Katya walked away to loosen up her muscles. Jessup chased her down the corridor. "What the fuck was that? You made it sound like you won this race for us."

"She did," MarKaln said. Terence nodded his agreement.

"She spread her legs for that genetic freak."

Katya glared at Jessup and turned away. She wasn't listening to this. He grabbed her arm and jerked her back. "When we go back out there — "

"Never touch her again."

Bach's soft deadly voice froze them all into position. Katya recovered first, stepping between Bach and Jessup, knowing Jessup would die if she didn't.

"I'm fine."

"He put his hands on you."

"I've had more than my hands on her," Jessup sneered. There was no way she could stop it. Bach set her aside and slammed his fist into Jessup's jaw. The team leader crumpled into a pile.

"She belongs to me now. And I will erase any memory she had of you."

The click-whir of multiple vid-cams activating put Jessup into performance mode. "Katya, honey, are you sure this is what you want? He's not human. What kind of life would you have? His kind are documented killers, barbarians. Imagine how they treat their women."

Bach tensed and she saw his fist rise again. She grabbed his arm before he could strike, using her weight to hold him back.

"Bach might not be pure-human, but he'd never sell me either."

Jessup thrust himself to his feet, glaring at her and keeping out of Bach's reach. "Fine, when we're done with this, go with him. Live in dirt huts with no tech and no running water. I don't care."

"I never thought you did."

"Two minutes," the hostess called, her voice sweet, her lips twitching with questions. "We need you in place."

MarKaln and Terence walked off. Jessup ignored Bach and tipped his head toward the set. Katya shook her head. "You have to. This is part of the agreement. You'll forfeit everything if don't complete the interviews."

She shook her head again. She was tired of it all. If she went back she'd have to pretend she didn't despise Jessup and she couldn't do it. She thought of the prize money she was giving up. It would have been nice but it wasn't worth it. She'd just have to keep working.

Jessup shrugged and grinned. "More for us then." He took his place on the set, explaining to the hostess that Katya wouldn't be joining them.

"Are you sure you want to do that?" Bach asked.

"Yes." A sudden wave of relief spiraled through her chest. This was the right decision. "What are you doing here?" she finally thought to ask. They'd left him miles away at the forest's edge. How had he found them?

"Jez met me at the forest edge and reminded me I'm not an idiot and it would be idiotic to let you go."

The statement left her breathless. "I don't know what to say."

"Say you'll stay. To see where this goes." He lifted her hand and placed a kiss in her palm. "I'm not the barbarian he says but he's right, I'm not fully human either."

She smiled. She'd seen glimpses of the animal side and knew the human struggled with that part of his personality but as a man—she'd never met his equal.

"I can handle it. I think."

His eyes glittered with the heat she'd grown used to.

"Come. I will take you to my lodgings."

Katya shivered as she followed him from the vid-set, partly from sexual anticipation, partly from the dread of the chilly room and cold wash water. What was she getting herself into?

Bach smiled at her as they walked into the sunlight and she knew it would be all right. He would keep her warm.

Epilogue

ഔ

Katya rolled over and groaned. Her body ached—deliciously. Since leaving the vid-set, Bach had been ravenous, demanding and awarding sexual pleasure beyond her wildest fantasies. She glanced around the room. The shining white furniture glowed in the evening sun. From the window, she could see the entire city. On the walk here, Bach had casually explained that he didn't live in a single-room hut but instead at the top of the tallest building in the city, situated at the edge of town, overlooking the forest his people protected.

Bach strolled into the room, his long blond hair loose and hanging down his back as he sank down onto the bed.

"Good evening," he said against her lips, kissing her breathless. She slid her fingers into his hair and held on, loving the sensual stroke to her skin. Early in the morning, as she cried out her hunger and need, he'd loosened the tie to his hair. Strangely, the implication didn't frighten her as it should. Bach groaned as she tugged on the thick strands. "Wait, kitten, I came in here for another reason. Jez buzzed through. They are re-showing yesterday's interviews. Said we should watch. Wall activate." The far wall lit up. The hostess smiled to the camera.

"We've had a slight change in personnel. Katya, who sacrificed herself to the Riabhians for safe passage through the forest, has left the team. So, we'll continue with the remaining members." She faced the team, smiling as the camera picked her up. "Team leader Jessup Starmart also had an exciting race." Jessup winked into the lens. "One night in the Riabhach Forest, the team was hosted by a creature from that world. I don't think you've seen this footage, Jessup."

The vid-cam stayed on Jessup's face as they showed clear footage of him and the two guards. His mouth dropped open as the vid showed him kneeling and sucking the guard's cock between his lips. Jessup's recorded groans echoed through the studio followed by the guard's harsh cry as he came in Jessup's mouth.

Bach shook his head. "I warned him not to drink anything."

"Well, it's good to know someone can get an orgasm from Jessup," she said.

Bach flipped her onto her back and rolled on top of her.

"You mean you never came with him?"

She shrugged. "I told you I could fake it."

Bach threw his head back and laughed. He pulled her to him and rolled onto his back. "I'll work hard to make sure you never have to."

Also by Tielle St. Clare

Christmas Elf

Close Quarters

Dragon's Fire

Dragon's Kiss

Dragon's Rise

Ellora's Cavemen: Legendary Tails II (*anthology*)

Enter the Dragon (*anthology*)

Irish Enchantment (*anthology*)

Just One Night

Simon's Bliss

Through Shattered Light

Transformations (*anthology*)

About the Author

Tielle (pronounced "teal") St. Clare has had lifelong love of romance novels. She began reading romances in the 7th grade when she discovered Victoria Holt novels and began writing romances at the age of 16 (during Trigonometry, if the truth be told). During her senior year in high school, the class dressed up as what they would be in twenty years—Tielle dressed as a romance writer. When not writing romances, Tielle has worked in public relations and video production for the past 20 years. She moved to Alaska when she was seven years old in 1972 when her father was transferred with the military. Tielle believes romances should be hot and sexy with a great story and fun characters.

Tielle welcomes comments from readers. You can find her website and email address on her author bio page at www.ellorascave.com

Why an electronic book?

We live in the Information Age—an exciting time in the history of human civilization, in which technology rules supreme and continues to progress in leaps and bounds every minute of every day. For a multitude of reasons, more and more avid literary fans are opting to purchase e-books instead of paper books. The question from those not yet initiated into the world of electronic reading is simply: *Why?*

1. ***Price.*** An electronic title at Ellora's Cave Publishing and Cerridwen Press runs anywhere from 40% to 75% less than the cover price of the exact same title in paperback format. Why? Basic mathematics and cost. It is less expensive to publish an e-book (no paper and printing, no warehousing and shipping) than it is to publish a paperback, so the savings are passed along to the consumer.

2. ***Space.*** Running out of room in your house for your books? That is one worry you will never have with electronic books. For a low one-time cost, you can purchase a handheld device specifically designed for e-reading. Many e-readers have large, convenient screens for viewing. Better yet, hundreds of titles can be stored within your new library—on a single microchip. There are a variety of e-readers from different manufacturers. You can also read e-books on

your PC or laptop computer. (Please note that Ellora's Cave does not endorse any specific brands. You can check our websites at www.ellorascave.com or www.cerridwenpress.com for information we make available to new consumers.)

3. *Mobility.* Because your new e-library consists of only a microchip within a small, easily transportable e-reader, your entire cache of books can be taken with you wherever you go.

4. ***Personal Viewing Preferences.*** Are the words you are currently reading too small? Too large? Too... ANNOYING? Paperback books cannot be modified according to personal preferences, but e-books can.

5. ***Instant Gratification.*** Is it the middle of the night and all the bookstores near you are closed? Are you tired of waiting days, sometimes weeks, for bookstores to ship the novels you bought? Ellora's Cave Publishing sells instantaneous downloads twenty-four hours a day, seven days a week, every day of the year. Our webstore is never closed. Our e-book delivery system is 100% automated, meaning your order is filled as soon as you pay for it.

Those are a few of the top reasons why electronic books are replacing paperbacks for many avid readers.

As always, Ellora's Cave and Cerridwen Press welcome your questions and comments. We invite you to email us at Comments@ellorascave.com or write to us directly at Ellora's Cave Publishing Inc., 1056 Home Avenue, Akron, OH 44310-3502.

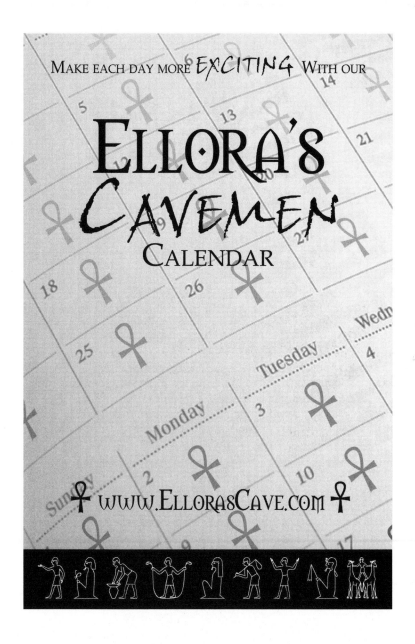

MAKE EACH DAY MORE *EXCITING* WITH OUR

ELLORA'S
CAVEMEN
CALENDAR

WWW.ELLORASCAVE.COM

erridwen, the Celtic Goddess of wisdom, was the muse who brought inspiration to story-tellers and those in the creative arts. Cerridwen Press encompasses the best and most innovative stories in all genres of today's fiction. Visit our site and discover the newest titles by talented authors who still get inspired - much like the ancient storytellers did, once upon a time.

Cerridwen Press

www.cerridwenpress.com